A FLOWER R

By Kirstin Graham

KIRSTIN
GRAHAM

To the love of my life, thank you for always believing in me, pushing me and reminding me that I can do whatever I set my mind to.

To my mother, grandmother and aunt: You are my heroes. You'll never stop inspiring me to do all I can no matter what.

I love you all.

It feels weird

No longer being in your shadow

With the sun hitting my face harshly

And the wind blowing me all over

I always thought I could be independent

That I'd be this confident energy when I was out of your shade

That nothing, nothing, could stop me being me

But now I seem to have lost part of me

I feel hollow

Empty

Alone

Even when I'm surrounded by people

Because none of them are you

And they never will be

PROLOGUE

She smouldered angrily as the flames wisped around the turf fire. She didn't belong here. With people like them. A dark shadow casted over her direction, blocking her view of the embers. The tall, balding man spoke, echoing in the trees.

"Welcome", he bellowed, "to your safe zone." She groaned, already bored, as her hair became her shield. As the empty promises surrounded all the participants, their eyes following his every movement, her eyes glanced back to the pit. Part of her was holding in the urge to put her hand into the glowing warmth. She wanted to feel the tickle on her fingertips, even if the pain hit shortly after. It made her feel closer to the reality she claimed to live in.

"Everything you say here is private," the counsellor continued, "and nothing will leave this campfire. Addictions. Abuse. Whatever has put you in your current predicament. Exhale. Inhale. Scream your issues. Take a step forward, let your soul out." He took his place back on the fold-out bench. No one moved.

"Good," she sighed to herself, "I'm not the only one who finds this bullshit." Counselling was not her idea of mending, especially not with a group of strangers. It was all because of her mother. She'd never met a pushier woman in her life. The phrase "I'm fine" sounded like "I'll never get over it" in dictator world, meaning for the weekend, Friday evening until Sunday afternoon at least, she was stuck with strange faces who didn't know her ordeal. Her emerald contacts glimmered in the light of the fire, disguising another scar from her past.

As if someone had suddenly adjusted his strings, pulling them tightly and rapidly, the counsellor sprang back to his feet, a grimace spreading from one side of the camp side to the other.

"Fine. If none of you want to speak aloud, then I guess it's time for Ice Breakers." The group was filled with murmurs, cursing and sulking faces. She smirked. Maybe she could make a friend or two, as rare as that was for her.

She still wished her mother had never noticed. If she hadn't, if her mother had only glanced at the marks and believed the excuses, she would still be in the comfort of her own home - surrounded by her collections, her multiple escapes, the ever-growing piles of unfinished projects. Why focus on reality when you can live in a fantasy? Why be yourself when you can be thousands of other characters? If she threw these questions at her mother, she'd be labelled as "weird" or "anti-social". It wasn't her fault no one understood, and she definitely couldn't find someone who'd understand here, even if these people had issues themselves.

"Azalea," she felt fifteen sets of eyes dart at her, the sudden attention causing her to blush furiously, "Why would you say you are here?" the counsellor inquired in what must have been his overly-rehearsed, approachable and caring voice. Her stomach spasmed with butterflies on a frenzy.

"I had no choice," she murmured as she looked around the group. Did all eyes really have to focus on her like that? "It was either here or be mithered to until my heart stops." She heard a few sniggers, giggles of agreement. No one ever wanted to be here, there was always a persistent family member behind it.

She felt the urge to continue speaking, but the black, monstrous dog that surrounded her wouldn't allow it. It still loomed over her thoughts, her anxiety, indulging itself on the happy moments whenever they presented themselves. A moment of confidence was a week-long banquet in her mind, served on the best silver platters, with embarrassment and self-loathing perched at the end of the table devouring the scraps. She couldn't imagine what would happen if she'd ever meet someone extraordinary, someone who could bring her out of her isolation, even just for a brief moment. An individual like that would cause more than just a panic inside her. She'd probably be committed afterwards, that was the next step after all.

Her eyes darted back to the flames. There was something pulling her back to it. As she focused on the flickers and sparks, her eyes became drawn to the individual behind them. The girl's freshly bleached hair remained perfectly straight, even with the wind sweeping through the trees. It hung beyond her waist, almost reaching the autumn leaves scattered around. Her pale face reminded Azalea of milk. Smooth, fresh and without a single taint in its colouring. Even with the cool air caressing the group, the girl's skin showed no reddening goosebumps longing for warmth. She shone radiantly in the fire's presence, as if without its light she may fade into the oblivion. Her own eyes appeared to be distant. She probably wished to be anywhere but here too.

It had been a few minutes, or maybe a few hours, before Azalea realized that the activity of the safe place she was trapped in was passing around her. Conversations had started up and she had no idea how long she'd been out of it, her mind escaping the invisible bars she was stuck in. She glanced back to the ghost girl to meet a set of golden eyes looking straight into her soul with an innocent smile appearing on the girl's lips. As her lips mouthed "hi", Azalea started to feel the butterflies again, hitting harder and heavier than before.

As the evening sky darkened to a pitch black abyss without a star in sight, the group's numbers shrank until there were only 2 around the fading embers of the fire pit. Azalea had adjusted to the silence as others disappeared to their tents and sleeping bags to the point she hadn't realized she still had company until she caught a slight motion out of the corner of her eye. Across from her remained the ghostly girl, with a cigarette dangling from between her skeletal fingers. The girl made no attempt to light it, even though she kept raising it to her lips before bringing it back down to her side. After a few minutes, she tore the cigarette up and threw its' remnants to the floor. As if she knew Azalea was watching her actions intently, she responded to the question just forming in her mind.

"I just quit," she shrugged nonchalantly, as if explaining herself was a common automatic response in her mind. She swept her hair neatly behind her left ear. "I'm Tabitha, but my non-existent friends call me Tabby." She held her hand across the ashes and waited for a hand in return. Azalea stared at the hovering hand for a moment too long, unsure what to do before Tabitha withdrew it. She rose to her feet, and started to head away before she turned back.

"Don't worry," she called as she found Azalea's eyes in the

surrounding darkness, "You'll be able to handle human touch again one day."

As the strange girl walked away, Azalea looked at the palm of her hand. The faint scar remained looming, running from her palm to her wrist where it met similar markings. The girl was wrong; she'd never be able to cope with anyone touching her ever again.

CHAPTER 1

Azalea woke up as the sun started to shine through the pale cream fabric embodying her. She felt as content with life as she usually did when entering the world of the living. For a moment, as brief as it was, she thought it was all a dream. That finally she'd returned from her nightmarish memories. The second she heard the whistling wind from outside her tent, and the other campers heavily stomping around like cattle, she snapped back to reality. Instead of the peaceful quiet that was her abode, she was in the great outdoors with other broken people. She rubbed the gunk out of her eyes and rolled to face her tent's entrance. She could face the day. She grumbled in despair as she untangled herself from what sleeping bag remained covering her. She hoped today would speed past her, just so she could return to the safety and sanity of her four walls at home tomorrow afternoon.

As she hovered around the pots of mildly warm breakfast food, trying to decide if the limp bacon or the undercooked sausage looked more edible, that pair of eyes found her across the campsite. She glanced up to see that in the natural light the eyes she'd found hard to get out of her mind were more hazel than gold, but they still had the same piercing effect. As Tabitha made her way over, Azalea's heart drummed frantically against her ribcage. She felt like a stage light was hovering, just beyond view, bringing all the unwanted attention to her current location. Before she had even had a chance to poke at the pan of beans that looked like no one had risked them, Tabitha was at her side, glowing as the sunlight bounced off her pale complexion. With her slender frame and long legs, she looked like a porcelain Barbie doll, just waiting in her pristine box. The only thing that didn't look like it was handcrafted to perfection by an artist was her hair, which now looked as though she hadn't had the chance to thoroughly comb it this morning.

"Good morning, Azalea," she smiled friendly, though making sure to keep a good amount of distance after her reaction to the possibility of physical interaction the night before, "Did you sleep well?"

Azalea gazed at her warily, unsure if she should respond honestly or sarcastically. After a hard deliberation, she gave into the response of a normal person. "I slept okay. How about you?"

"Well, it could have been a lot worse. The freezing ground isn't exactly in my top ten sleeping places." Tabitha's smile widened, with her pearly whites in full view. The way she was looking at Azalea made her nervous, almost as if she were standing across from an anaconda with its' jaw unhinged, ready to swallow her whole. "It beats sleeping in a coffin though." Tabitha's expression briefly changed, ever so subtly, and it seemed as if the entire universe darkened for that moment. She cleared her throat and the smile returned, covering her true feelings like a mask. "So, what do you usually do for fun when you're not sat around with the mentally deranged?"

Azalea felt an uncontrollable tug at her lips as the smile escaped through them, followed by a nervous laugh she didn't recognize as her own. "Usually, I'm sat by myself doing nothing, so I'm still with someone mental no matter where I go." She watched as Tabitha's true smile returned to her full mouth with her small, piercing cackle of laughter clashing against the border of trees engulfing them. Part of her longed to extend the conversation more, but the rest of her, her anxious side included, felt like she was already walking on eggshells. She felt the usual storm start inside of her as her lungs began to feel heavy and her thoughts started to scramble. She didn't want to have a panic attack. Not here. She already felt like she stood out, she didn't need to be marked as a pathetic loser any more than she already was.

One. Two.

The countdown ticked away automatically, her mind always prepared as if it were still the aftermath, where the slightest thing would set her off. "Fight the panic, Az!" she demanded of herself.

Three. Four. Five.

The feeling of being out of her depth started to wash over her, drowning her alive with her attempts of normality. "Control it, don't react to it, you're still alive!"

Six.

The anxiety began pulling her down like a dead weight, further and further away from the end of her episode. "You're safe; no one is going to hurt you."

Seven. Eight.

No matter how hard she tried, she struggled endlessly to resurface, still unable to breathe in the air her lungs desired. "You're stronger than this! Don't give in!"

Nine. Ten.

Her mind screaming and pleading for survival or salvation, whichever came first, finally loosened Azalea from her anxiety enough for her to take a step back to reality, her countdown blaring like a police siren intensified by the quiet.

Eleven. Twelve.

As her internal countdown finally hit its marker, she gasped for breath. The worst part of her panic attacks was her loss of control, to feel like your body was failing the simplest of tasks, as if keeping herself alive became a massive ordeal and her organs didn't know how to respond. As her eyelashes fluttered rapidly, Tabitha's look of concern came more into focus.

"Are you okay?" She curiously pursued as she looked over Azalea, her focus drawn to her heaving chest, still noticeably trying to get itself together. She reached out to touch her arm in an effort to comfort her before recalling the night before. "I'll get you something to drink." With a mere nod in response, Tabitha walked towards the cooler containing bottles of water. By the time she'd turned back to return to Azalea's side, she was gone.

She didn't know why she ran. The uncomfortable, overwhelming urge to hide away from her issues had instinctively flooded her and set her in motion. A few steps turned into a few more, and before she knew it she was standing on a riverbed, watching the steady waves slapping against the scattered rocks submerged throughout its course. If only she could be one with the river, forever flowing and never ending, washing away all the bad entities in its' way. Her heart still racing, she groaned angrily to herself. She thought the panic attacks were gone.

It had been so long since her last one, the memory of it appeared distorted in her mind. Her mother's tired face as she sighed heavily, packing the last of the boxes into the attic to remain there until no one remembered they ever existed. The empty room, reflecting exactly how she felt inside. The sound of a pin drop would have been vastly amplified by its' four walls. Staring into the room looking so bare, the unbearable guilt washed over her. Suddenly, she felt as if she were covered head to toe in 2 inches of dirt and rushed to the bathroom to rub her skin raw with a scrubbing brush. After an hour in the shower, removing layer after layer of herself, she finally broke down and cried until her throat tightened, her inhaling becoming frantic as she gasped for oxygen. Every inch of her was losing control. The room started to fade into pure darkness. Her last memory from before she blacked out was that of her mother, breaking through the door as she lay curled in a ball at the bottom of the cubicle, screaming bloody murder as if she had just lost her world all over again. The day after, she awoke in a hospital bed covered in wires and tubes. Her mother was asleep at her side, gripping tightly to her right arm as it hung over the bed's frame. She lay there, watching her mother finally resting, unable to move without being stabbed deeper by the needles stuck into her left arm, connecting her to an IV.

She was stuck in that room for three days, being tested like a lab rat, whilst they ruled out major illnesses and diseases to satisfy her mother's paranoia. It took another two days for her to be diagnosed with anxiety and depression, while her mother informed the medical staff that "It wasn't much of a surprise" after noticing the barely healing wounds on her wrists. Her self-mutilation wasn't a suicide attempt by any means, as much as her mother probably assumed it was. It was her way of being in control of her life, and her future, even if it only lasted the few moments the razor blade slashed into her flesh. She had the power to stop it, but the physical pain at least eased the mental burdens she felt for those few seconds before she realized she'd overstepped her boundaries once again. Whilst she longed to control her mind, she didn't wish to die. She knew it would kill her mother to lose a member of her brood in such a selfish way.

It had been four months, two weeks and three days since her last panic attack, and another five days on top of that since she last used her skin as a carving platter. After her hostile hospital in-patient stay, her mother was issued antidepressants for Azalea as it was felt amongst the staff and her mother, who remained her legal guardian and owner for another 5 months, that she could not be trusted with her own medication for the time being. At home all of the pills that were once stored in the kitchen and bathroom cabinets, including the child strength ibuprofen, were locked away for her safety.

"I don't want to lose you any time soon," her mother argued as Azalea accused her of trying to control her entire existence. "I'm doing all of this for your own good!" Her mother even went out of her way to contact an old family friend who worked with troubled teenagers to see if there was any way to get Azalea "the help she needed". There was no reasoning with her when Felicity 'Feather' Grace Hart, Hippy-turned-overprotective Pitbull, was trying to solve the world's problems. To stop World War III from blasting off in her front room one evening in mid-January, she reluctantly agreed to start counselling with Lucy, a late-twenties woman who resembled a shrew in many ways. After just three sessions with the obnoxious twit that was Lucy, Azalea was pleading with her mother for any other option.

"Maybe group counselling will be better for you if you can't handle the one to one sessions with a counsellor," her mother said, grabbing her tablet and starting yet another search for professionals Azalea didn't want or need in her life, "You never know, your peers might bring you back out of that shell of yours."

As she sat at the riverbed with the smooth waves lapping against her toes, Azalea's stomach rumbled angrily, waiting for sustenance. She sighed, defeated. She hadn't eaten since yesterday and there was no way she could skip another camp meal without the counsellor sending out a search party. She left her feet dangling into the cool water for a few moments more before pulling them to her side and kicking them into her pumps.

Walking back towards the campsite, Azalea took in the picturesque surroundings. The bluebells scattered in the shadows of the Birch trees, the purple orchids painted perfectly in the brush. It was almost like being inside a living postcard scene, encircled by its' beauty. If it weren't for her allergies, she'd happily remain in the woodlands for eternity, but her eyes and nose starting to leak reminded her that she needed civilization to survive. As she got closer to the campgrounds, the flowers became few and far between, their innocent aroma being overwhelmed by the smoke lacing its' way between the treetops and clouds. From her path, Azalea could see the small groups of teens with the counsellor moving around them, as if he was choosing who to ambush with an unnecessarily awkward conversation next. With the snap of a twig under her size 4 pump, her quiet approach became a spectacle for all to gawk at.

"Ah, Miss Hart," the counsellor smiled across the camp at her, "we were wondering if you'd be back in time for our planned activities." He walked around the groups, gesturing to the sheets of paper they all had in front of them. She glanced at the papers. It looked like they were doing mind maps, with words scribbled all over the pages from the tiniest of squiggles to the largest of scratchings. Either he set up the groups based on their issues or whatever system he used to place people together to work was flawless.

"As you and Tabitha appear to be close already, why not join her?" Azalea's eyes darted from the counsellor to Tabitha, who was staring at her group's sheet intently to avoid the glares in her direction. She headed to the group, her eyes drawn to their sheet. Three words stood out, practically etched into the ground it lay on. Grief. Guilt. Abuse. She glanced at Tabitha, whose eyes remained unmoving from the page. Maybe they had more in common than Azalea had originally thought.

Not a word was uttered between the pair for the rest of that afternoon, or a glance shared. Whilst the rest of their group continued with the tasks at hand, an awkward air hung around the duo. Azalea stared at the boy next to her, Tony if she remembered correctly, as he added a few more items to his list. The current task was to write down all their negative feelings and thoughts for the bonfire later. They were set to torch their lists alight to clear their minds of all the darkness. The latest fad, it seemed, to cross the covers of Counsellor Weekly. Her own list consisted of a total of six words. Poppy. Dad. Halloween. Scars. Memories. Existence. Every word triggered thousands of bad thoughts to flash across her mind in neon lights, Poppy sparking off the most disturbing thoughts of all. She couldn't even think of what else to note down, so many things set off her mind.

Her eyes darted to everyone's sheets. Tony's page was almost full and the other two were already writing on the back of theirs.

Tabitha hadn't even picked up her pen. It just lay in front of her with her paper being hit limply by the wind. Every time it looked like she was about to reach out for the pen, her hand would linger above it for a moment before returning to her lap. Azalea understood how hard it could be to write your feelings down, but she remained curious as to what could be haunting Tabitha so thoroughly. Her expression showed whatever was on her mind was embedded so deeply that no matter what she wrote on the flimsy sheet of lined paper that lay before her, it would only touch the surface of how she felt inside. Maybe, just maybe, Tabitha could be someone to turn to for the remaining night they were outside the city's borders Azalea thought to herself. The activities left her feeling vulnerable, and any small comforts would be better than being isolated until she could return home once more. She must have felt she was being watched, as Tabitha's eyes met Azalea's. A faint smile appeared on Tabitha's lips, as if she knew exactly how Azalea felt at that moment. Azalea felt her own face smile back at this stranger, the one she could feel herself warming to. She watched as Tabitha finally picked up the pen and started working on her own list. At first her hand moved slowly and gracefully across the page, but as she could be seen really getting into her work, the movement became rapid, as if every word demanded to be written at the exact moment it formed in her mind. She watched as Tabitha's writing curved and curled to fit every inch of the paper it could reach. She was unsure if she'd watched for only seconds, or hours, but before she knew it the counsellor was calling back their attention to the centre of the camp, where he was about to light the campfire.

"Okay," he called amongst the groups, "I think that should have been enough time to get a good list. I'll call you up one by one once I've got the fire started to burn your papers." Whilst he struggled to get the turf to light, the groups started talking amongst themselves. What were their plans for when they returned home. Where they lived. What they do for work and fun. The standard small talk questions you'd hear anywhere felt unusual in their current setting. Surrounded by woodlands and nature didn't feel like the type of location where you discuss such impersonal matters, especially if you've been dragged out of the city by a counsellor with zero wilderness skills. From the corner of her eye, Azalea saw Tabitha tear her paper and tuck half of it away inside her hoodie's pocket. Just as the words were forming in her mouth, the flames burst from the pile of turf with the counsellor looking victorious by its' side. "Right, let's begin!"

One by one, the teenagers were summoned to the side of the fire, being watched intently by the counsellor, to place their lists into its' blazing mouth. As the pages crumbled into ash, a rush of relief appeared to hit its' owner's lips before they took their seats again to watch the next participant. As her name was hollered, she rose to her feet, anxious to get it over and done with. Her list repeated in her mind, floating past faster and faster until they were catching her off-guard at the blink of an eye. Dad. Existence. Memories. Poppy. Halloween. Scars. Memories. Poppy. Scars. Poppy. Poppy. Poppy. It was as if her brain had hit repeat when it came to her. Poppy just kept repeating, even as she placed her list into the flames. There was no rush of ease, just a longing to be anywhere but here. As she watched her list burn, she felt the urge once more to thrust her hand into the fiery touch of the campfire but she resisted, aware she was being watched from all around. She swallowed her urges, took the eight steps away to where she was sat and sunk back to the ground. As the last few people took their turns, she fought her brain, pushing those thoughts back into the darkness where she wanted them to remain.

CHAPTER 2

As the colours of the afternoon faded into the evening's light, the group was full of laughter and smiles. It was as if most of their burdens had disappeared into the pile of ashes under the campfire's flame. Azalea sat lonesome on a log, distancing herself from the rest. Her mind was no longer in overdrive but she feared the closer she got to the flames and the remnants of the list she created, the easier it would be to lose control again. Her eyes were so intensely glued to the ground beneath her feet, she didn't even notice the movement to her right.

Tabitha sat on a dry pile of leaves, her arm resting on Azalea's perch, mere inches from her uncovered thigh. She did not speak, nor did she face Azalea. Her glowing eyes were drawn to the rest of the group as they appeared to be having the time of their lives. Their cheeriness seemed to spread from one to the other like the sparks that fluttered in the breeze around the fire's embers. Tabitha's proximity to her bare skin made her tense up nervously. It had been a different lifetime when she had last felt anyone's warmth near such an area of her body. She inched slowly away from the arm, her mind memorizing the little freckles that appeared to play dot to dot over Tabitha's elbow and bicep. As the log rolled forward a centimetre under Azalea's movement, it drew Tabitha's attention to her face which soon began to fill with crimson. Embarrassed, she turned to look away from the girl whose eyes she felt glancing at her back. "Hey," came the voice from behind her, "How are you feeling?"

She shrugged, unable to get the words off the tip of her tongue at that moment. No words in the English language seemed to sum up exactly how she felt. The numbness she had coursing through her body may have been something she was used to, but she was never able to attach it to one emotion. She just felt empty. She turned to look at Tabitha to see her nodding in response. Of course she understood, she was just as broken herself, she'd just had more practice.

"Yeah, I get that," Tabitha smiled, "the pit's always hard to claw your way back out of when you're in deep, but you'll get there." A few loose strands of her blonde hair blew into her face, tickling her cheeks. She quickly swept them behind her ear once more, smoothing the rest of her hair with her palms. Her face appeared so delicate up close, as if a light pressure on its' surface would shatter it.

"How do you do it?" The question unexpectedly came out of her mouth so fast, if it wasn't her voice that asked it Azalea would have sworn there was a third party in their conversation. "How do you keep going?" The question had plagued her mind for months, but this was the first time she'd asked it aloud. She knew any answer given by her mother or the team of specialist counsellors she called would be generic; impersonal; aiming to keep her alive. She longed to know how someone similar to herself could survive, and now was the perfect opportunity to ask.

A faint chuckle erupted from Tabitha. "I take it all a day at a time. I couldn't handle more than that." She glanced at Azalea, and half-heartedly smiled. "Sometimes it's better to live in the moment than focus on the past." She reached out and offered her hand to Azalea once more. "Let's start afresh. Hi, I'm Tabby."

Azalea fought the urge to flee from the touch and reached out to shake Tabitha's hand. "I'm Az." As their hands shook in the fire light, one confident and the other sweating profusely, the campfire crackled, growing dimmer as the hours passed.

The girls remained by each other's side for the rest of the evening, into the early hours of the morning, discussing anything and everything they could think of. It was the first time in a long while that she felt like she had a friend and Azalea didn't want that moment to end. By the time they finally stumbled into their individual tents to catch a few hours of shut eye, she felt as if Tabitha - Tabby - could be a friendly shoulder to turn to in her hours of need. They'd already exchanged their numbers and email addresses to make sure they could keep in touch. Tabby lived two hours away by train, so it wasn't as if they'd just run into each other out in public on a regular basis.

"Finally," Azalea sighed to herself as she lay under the light sleeping bag she'd flung aside earlier that morning. It smelt like nature, causing her nose to turn up in distain. She couldn't help imagining her warm, embracing bed at home, with its' mattress that curved perfectly to the shape of her spine, and the goose feather pillows plumped to perfection tucked under her silk sheets. Just a dozen more hours and then she'd be back within her comfort zone, surrounded by her many escapes. Within minutes of her head touching the soft pillow of her sleeping bag, her eyes closed, darkening her vision until nothing remained.

It may have been minutes later, or even hours as the concept of time was nonexistent, but the pitch black land in which she usually dreamt gradually filled with a crimson sky with a storm hovering a stone's throw away in the distance. It had been months since her dreams had any colour, and that was for the best. The colours her mind summoned when she was unable to control it haunted her in the waking hours. She stood, her feet glued to the floor with fear, wearing an outfit she had torched months prior, hoping to escape this nightmare. Her fingers traced the intricate embroidery she had designed and sewn by hand for weeks on end, grazing against the lace around the corset. The velvet feel against her bare arms was turning her stomach. The skirt swept with the wind, the chiffon underlayer scratching against her thighs. She hated every little detail she remembered adding to this one of a kind costume. All the time she'd spent on it, praising her own design and craftsmanship, twirling around the front room to show her mother just how perfect she looked. She was all ready for another Halloween evening watching scary movies alone, dressed to the nines, with a cauldron of snacks waiting for trick or treaters. She glanced around her, evaluating her environment, to discover her front door 3 metres from her left. The traditional decorations for the season donned the steps. Jack o' lanterns, with a wire, rusty black cat perched next to them. A witch's hat hanging from the nail that remained there year round just to be used for their Christmas wreath. The hangman's empty noose swinging from the tree by the kitchen window. She urged herself to run in the opposite direction, but her feet remained rooted to the floor.

As the storm drew closer, enveloping the sky until the reds turned to grey, the screams began. At first, the sounds were faint, but as the storm approached with its' thundering clouds, they grew in volume. As the first lightning bolt crashed to the earth, the screeching became more crystal, the inaudible mumblings becoming clearer as the cumulonimbus clouds approached. "Azalea!" The blood-curdling voice echoed, "Help!" Her feet, seeming to move of their own accord, started towards the thunder and lightning. The screams of her name got louder, as did the pleas for help. There was nothing she could do, she knew, but all of her wanted to run to safety and prevent it happening all over again.

The storm instantly engulfed her, making her the centre of its' attention. The clouds started to glow as they swirled around her, twisting and twirling until they formed a barrier, entrapping her from the rest of the world. Every cry, moan and whimper seemed amplified. She screwed her eyes shut, willing her body to wake up. She needed reality; she needed sanity; she needed to be anywhere but here. No matter how hard she tried, it didn't work. As tears starting streaming down her face, she felt droplets hit her scalp. Opening her eyes and lightly swiping and the wet mess that had started to coat her, she became speechless. It wasn't rain. She started to whimper as she dropped to her knees, in pure shock. A puddle was forming next to her, blood red and thicker than water. "Poppy," the cry escaped her, as her body started to shake. She pleaded with her mind to free her and as the final scream bellowed from above, it granted her wish.

Her eyes burst open, darting around the shadowed space around her. Nothing out of place. Nothing out of order. She was alone. The screaming had stopped and there was only the sound of the neighbouring snores in the background. The sleeping bag clung to her sweaty skin, soaking it thoroughly. She felt the urge to scrub the nightmares away. Flinging the wet sleeping bag aside, she jumped to her feet and shoved her toes into her slippers. The shower was calling her. She hastily grabbed her overnight bag and towel and kicked her way out of the tent, leaving the door flapping lightly in the breeze.

The sun had started to rise over the hills in the distance, erupting the sky with a magnificent orange, casting its' light far across the surroundings. Everything the light touched appeared to glow momentarily, flush with brightness. She sleepily staggered towards the shower building, her beauty products in hand. As her eyes began to itch, she wiped at them rapidly before cursing herself under her breath. She hadn't removed her contacts, no wonder her eyes hurt. Sleeping in them was a big mistake. Opening the door to the shower building, she headed directly to the mirror, prepared to see the worst.

Sweeping up the mess she called her hair, she stared at her mirror self. As she feared, her eyes were swollen. A side effect to sleeping with flimsy plastic layers covering her sensitive corneas. With pure motivation, she had the lenses out and cleaning in solution within a matter of minutes. Looking at her reflection, she viewed it with scorn. Her right eye was bloodshot beyond recognition whilst her left eye appeared to have reacted less. She didn't even know if it was possible for her blind eye to get bloodshot with how many nerves were cauterized as her eye was reconstructed. She was lucky enough she was alive, she didn't feel like asking those types of silly questions when she was in the hospital. They'd slipped from her mind anyway in the long run, the only thing that mattered at that point was her breathing lungs. She felt the urge to cry at that point, seeing herself as herself after so long. She'd almost perfectly avoided her reflection over the last few months that it caused her a fright every time she glanced upon herself. She felt like Quasimodo without her made up image, scared the villagers will flee from her in their presence, or even worse publicly display her as the monster she was for the entire world to see.

Her remaining sky blue eye seemed to haunt her as it looked back at her from the mirror. Ignoring it, she rummaged in her packed overnight bag for her other set of contacts. She'd brought the only spares she had available at hand before she left, thinking she wouldn't need to resort to them. Bright purple. She sighed angrily before placing them lightly under her eye lids, blinking a few times to adjust to their placement. Once her eyes were ready, she yanked the pair of swimming goggles from the bag and placed them securely.

The swimming goggles became a necessity when she first decided to shower whilst wearing the contact lenses. An attempt of wearing them without eye coverage in the shower proved difficult when the contact became uncomfortable and she nearly crashed through the glass screen. She always thought she'd be able to shower without needing them, but after being caught without her contacts in a few times by family members who seemed to have forgotten her ordeal, it just seemed easier to explain why she was wearing swimming equipment to shower than it did explaining why one of her eyes was permanently tinted white. Picking the first cubicle she approached, she pulled the sickly green shower curtain behind herself, enjoying the moment of privacy she had before anyone else woke.

Welcoming the caress of the warm water on her scalp and skin, Azalea scrubbed the remnants of the sweat and dirt from her fleshy surface, allowing the refreshing steam to intoxicate her senses. She lathered herself head to toe, soap bubbles everywhere, and stood still under the shower's powerful stream, letting it course over her skin at its' own pace, not wanting to return to the cold air outside of the shower's vicinity. Whilst she ran the shampoo and conditioner through her light brown hair, she heard a commotion outside the shower building door. Turning the shower off, footsteps could be heard clicking on the floor's tiles as someone approached. Not wanting to appear like a weirdo wearing swimming goggles in the shower to a group of her peers, Azalea quickly held her breath, hoping the other person would leave without noticing.

Her silence worked against her as within a moment of the footsteps stopping, a hand yanked open the curtain that shielded her dignity. She let out a squeal of embarrassment as a gasp of shock filled the air. "Shit," a male voice cursed as they turned to face the wall away from her, "I am so, so sorry. I didn't realize there was anyone in here." Azalea pulled the curtain back across whilst she reached for her towel that she had hung over the cubicle's top. Wrapping it around herself, and tucking it under her arms, she swiftly removed her goggles before opening the curtain again.

"How dare you!" Azalea screeched, holding the urge to slap the idiotic man who now stood by the sinks. "Did you not think someone was in there, with it being pulled shut?" She couldn't believe someone could be dumb enough to just open a shower curtain without asking aloud first if there was someone there. Had common courtesy died?

"I'm sorry," the botherer bumbled, "I didn't think... I thought it was empty, I was wrong." His eyes were glued to the floor, relieving Azalea. Maybe he hadn't seen as much as she thought.

"Who even are you?" She glared, "I thought the entire campsite was rented out to my group, and you are definitely not one of us." She slowly approached her pile of dirty clothes and grabbed her pajama bottoms. Whilst trying to remain balanced, she slipped one leg after the other into her clothes, keeping her eyes on the mysterious male.

"Just the camp's unpaid help," he mumbled lightly, his cheeks flushing crimson, "Honestly. I didn't know. Please, forgive me." His light grey eyes finally glanced up at her, filling instantly with relief that she was mostly covered. "I'm sorry if my idiotic behaviour ruined your visit."

Sighing, Azalea's eyes met the stranger's. His limp blonde hair hung over his thick eyebrows. His lips shook slightly, his nerves clearly getting to him. "It's okay. It happened. We can move on from it." She fought the urge to projectile vomit as she spoke the phrases often uttered by her old counsellor. Even the thought of those words filled her with the urge to scream and cry all at once. Some things were harder to move on from, and she knew it firsthand. "Just make sure you don't do it again, some girls might give you more than just verbal abuse."

The man half-heartedly chuckled. "I'll bear that in mind in the future. I don't want to be assaulted by naked people." As Azalea's chuckling joined his own, his eyes connected with hers. "If you want to make a complaint though, I'm sure my mum will appreciate it. She needs a new reason to shout at me. Just say 'Laine was an absolute nob' before you leave, and that'll keep her fueled up for a year."

Pulling her towel tightly around her chest, she smirked. "Can't I just be honest and call you a perv?" As the word 'perv' hung in the air, Laine's chest erupted with laughter.

"That's not the worst thing I've been called in this lifetime, and I'm sure even she's heard worse about me. Be honest all you like!" He smirked back as he grabbed the mop and bucket from the far corner of the room. Walking back into her cubicle, Azalea pulled the curtain across once more. She swiftly yanked her pajama top over her head and chest, making sure she was fully covered, before resurfacing from behind the plastic barrier. She grabbed everything of hers she could see scattered on the sink and forced it back into her overnight bag.

"I'll leave you to do your cleaning," she called as she left the shower block in a hurry, her belongings tucked under her right arm. She heard a response but chose to carry on, wanting to be as far away from that awkward situation as possible.

Returning to her tent, Azalea sighed. It was time to pack away everything she had brought. As much as she wished she was at home, part of her didn't want to return to her normal life, hiding away in the shadows of her practically vacant existence. She knew her loneliness would eat her up within a matter of days.

There was nothing worse than trying to fight the solitude when it was all she knew. The only companionship she would have when she returned to her humble abode was her two cats: her Toyger Dali and her Ragdoll Storm. She'd missed having them curled at her feet, fighting over which one could be tickled by her toes that night. Whilst their love and affection meant the world to her, she knew she couldn't rely on it forever. One day, even her cats would leave her.

Rolling up her sleeping bag, she imagined returning to her bed, cats in tow. They were the only reason home still felt like a place to go back to. It had been so awkward with her mother for the last few months; the cats were her only solace. With their bright blue eyes and their fluffy tails, they constantly pleaded their human mother for attention at all hours of the day. It left her no time to think of the trail of darkness that appeared to follow her through every chapter of her life's story. She shoved the remainder of her objects into her rucksack, hoping it would all fit. It had taken her hours of rearranging her bag before she left for this camp, and she didn't feel she had the patience to play Tetris with her belongings before eating. Roughly pulling the zip into its' resting place she let out a sigh of relief. She was finally ready to go home, her inner darkness in tow.

Heading towards the final breakfast buffet she would warily eat, a faint smile crept on her face. As bad as she thought the trip would be, it was tolerable for a weekend. She wouldn't have to return again, unless her mother felt it was "right" or "working". The only good thing that appeared to come out of the experience was meeting Tabby. Just thinking about her caused her heart to race. She felt so nervous, even without her presence nearby. There may have been embarrassing moments, a nightmare that soaked her through and a panic attack, but she could move on from it and keep living her life, hopefully with a new friend for the ride. Living is all she had planned for her future, anything else was just extra.

The activities of the morning and early afternoon flew by, Azalea practically glued to Tabitha's side. They spent all morning in whispers and murmurs, making sure they'd be able to keep in touch in the real world. It was as if they'd known each other for eternity, with many secrets hidden away between the pair. Never had she ever felt so alive until that moment. As they spoke, they learnt little by little what made up the other person, though there was an obvious block on the reasons that had brought them to the camp that weekend.

"I'm glad I met you," Tabby smiled happily at Azalea as they toasted their juice cartons during a short break. Tabby laid her head on the ground, the grass sticking up around her hair. The birch trees' branches hung overhead, with the faint sound on the river in the background. "I'm not really the 'friend' type back in civilization."

"No shit," She smiled back, "I don't think anyone who's here has any." She slurped from her carton giddily, enjoying the sun as it hit her back through a break in the foliage. The spot appeared to be more beautiful today than it was when she was last there on her own. The flowers seemed to be more fragrant and the sound of the river played tranquilly into their ears. "At least we know each other now." She looked over at Tabby then; staring at the palest skin she may ever see. Her eyes were closed, as if she were enjoying the serenade nature was playing for just them. Azalea wished she could take a picture and remember that moment forever. The moment she finally found a companion in life that left her truly at ease to be her own person, no lies or trickery.

"It'd be a catastrophe, that's for sure," Tabby agreed, eyes still glued shut. "Everyone I knew pre-disaster burnt their bridges with me, so other than me, myself and I, I don't really have anyone. Just my work colleagues and an old man who thinks I'm someone else."

"No parents?" Azalea found herself asking. She wished she could take the words back the millisecond they were traced out by her tongue. "Sorry," she immediately blushed focusing on Tabby's reaction. Tabby just shrugged, eyes still shut, as if she heard it a million times before. "I can't control my mouth or brain sometimes, it just blurts out."

"Don't worry about it," Tabby responded. "I often forget most people our age still have parents. Mine died years ago now. So I guess I'm an orphan. The only relative I have now is my grandpa and his Alzheimer's basically means no one remembers me." She tutted to herself, an abrupt laugh escaping suddenly, startling the nearby birds. "A child of the system, no wonder I'm so broken."

Azalea couldn't help but let out a laugh herself. Everyone present at the camp was broken for some reason or other, but everyone else seemed to be so bottled up, just like how she still was. Tabby on the other hand appeared to not give a damn about what happened in her past and could laugh about it. It was inspiring to know that somewhere down the line, maybe her past wouldn't cause her to seek the closest blade to hand. Maybe it wouldn't want to make her track down the bastard who broke her like this and push glass into his eye sockets. She'll be over it, and living with it, just like every other person deals with their problems, no panic attacks on the horizon.

Tabby pushed herself off the floor and held her hand out for Azalea, "We should head back. Need a hand?" Fighting her instinct to flee, Azalea took her hand and forced herself to stand. Holding onto Tabby's hand a few seconds too long once she was on her feet, she felt herself blushing again.

"Let's go," Azalea smiled back at Tabby, heading back towards the camp site, Tabby following behind her.

"The purple contacts suit you, by the way." Tabby called ahead to Azalea. So much had happened since that morning, Azalea had completely forgotten her eyes were an unnatural shade. She didn't know how to respond, so she remained quiet for a moment. "Want to sing a campfire song?" Azalea teased, humming the tune to Boa Constrictor as loud as she could. A squeal of "Fuck no" filled the spot they'd abandoned as they walked away.

Chapter 3

Upon returning to the camp site, Azalea glimpsed across the now vacant area to find Laine, assisting the counsellor in returning the folded tents into their store cupboards. He looked so happy, even if he was stuck helping a man with no personality. Following her eye, Tabby cooed.

"Who is *that*? I would have definitely noticed if *he* was with our group, wouldn't you?" Approaching the remainder of the fire pit, her eyes never left Laine's body, scanning from top to bottom. Her gaze seemed to infuriate Azalea's insides. Was she jealous? She asked herself curiously. She had no reason to be. She wasn't attracted to him; he appeared too simple for her own tastes. As Tabby's gaze lingered on the man, she decided to answer the rhetorical questions that hung in the air.

"He's the owner's son, or that's what he told me this morning." Azalea plopped herself on the log nearest the campfire, glancing at her new friend to see if she'd follow. She didn't. She remained stood, as if she didn't want to lose a moment of staring at Laine.

"And here I thought you didn't speak to men," Tabby smirked, finally looking back to Azalea. "When did you meet him then? And what's his name? Is he single? Does he like blondes or brunettes? Coke or Pepsi?" She giggled, trying to think of more irrelevant questions to ask.

"Damn, Tabby, I didn't ask him for his life story. He accidentally caught me a bit naked when I was showering this morning. My main thought was 'what the fuck'. All I know is his name is Laine, and he doesn't really think before pulling shower curtains open." Azalea murmured, that moment of embarrassment now on a loop in her head. It was over and done with; she didn't want to replay her humiliation any more times in her mind. Her cheeks shone red, whilst an obvious anger filled her eyes.

Tabby's smirk faded. "Shit, I'm so sorry, Az. I know that must have been hard for you. Are you okay?" Her face flooded with concern as she squatted down to Azalea's level, hovering at a slight distance. Azalea let out a huff of annoyance, and shrugged.

"It was embarrassing, but I can't say it's the worst thing to ever happen to me, can I?" She pulled her hair from behind her hair and started to loosely plait it, ignoring Tabby's proximity. She wanted to focus on something else, anything else. Any distraction would be better than nothing.

After a few attempts of plaiting and unplaiting her a few strands of hair, she was handed a zippo lighter with a T scratched on its' surface. "If you want to fidget, lighters are always fun. Fire is the best, after all." Tabby smiled, trying to gain Azalea's attention once more. Azalea let a faint smile cross her face as she opened and closed the lighter. As she went to hand it back, Tabby shook her head. "No, you can keep it, honestly." Her smile grew, "At least this way I know you'll remember me after this weekend."

"Thanks," Azalea smiled looking into Tabby's eyes, "though I doubt I'll ever forget you. Especially if we actually keep in contact."

The camp rustled with activity as the camp members packed up their possessions into the hired coach set to take them back to the local town. Laine swept out the fire pits, Tabby glancing at his perfect rump as he bent over. The counsellor was walking around, patting the shoulders of the teens as they tried to avoid his contact as much as they could. Azalea inhaled deeply, enjoying the last few moments of her camping experience before climbing into the coach and curling up for the long journey ahead of her. As the other campers joined her, waiting for their departure, she caught a glimpse of Tabby and Laine giggling as pieces of paper were exchanged. Looking away, she could feel the jealousy eating at her once again.

"Before I let you off the coach," the counsellor bellowed through the microphone as they pulled up outside of the local train station, "Just a few reminders: Firstly, contact me if you feel like you need to discuss anything, and we'll arrange some sessions for you in your local area with either myself or one of my team mates. Secondly, remember to care for yourselves. You are great teenagers and you all have a bright future ahead of you. Finally, confide in others. Don't bottle all of your issues up. That's what usually leads to breakdowns." Looking from face to face, the counsellor smiled sadly. "We can all heal ourselves; we just need to work on it step by step. I've been Matt, your counsellor for the weekend. I hope you all get home safe."

Peeling off the bus, one by one, the counsellor handed back out the small plastic bags containing their mobiles. Finally, Azalea thought, instantly unsealing the bag and scrolling through her phone. As usual, she had no notifications but she didn't care. All she wanted was a reminder of her feline children, calling her home. Two more hours by train and foot and she'd be home again, or as close as she could get to a home. Looking up from the pictures of her bundles of joy, she caught a glimpse of Tabby walking towards a taxi. As she watched the girl who caused such weird reactions in her leaving for what could only be a perfect existence, she sighed heavily. Maybe one day they will see each other again, only fate could decide.

Pulling her backpack closely to her shoulder she headed into the empty train station, griping her phone tightly in her right hand. Just as she queued to buy her ticket home, she felt her hand vibrate. Glancing at the screen, she felt her heart skip a beat. There, under an unknown number was a sentence she did not expect to see.

Until we meet again, smile for me. T x

Against her control, her lips obeyed the text message, her cheeks sore from just how much she had spent blushing in the last seventy-two hours. Grabbing her train ticket, she rushed to the platform, unsure of exactly how to respond to the text. Was it flirty? Was it friendly? Words were hard; confusing. She struggled with social interaction as it was, but text messaging took her anxiety to a whole new level. After stumbling over her own feet one too many times due to her lack of focus, she perched herself on a bench waiting for the train's arrival. Fuck it, she thought, tapping at her phone's keyboard frantically, wanting to get the unbearable moment over and done with. Hitting send she looked back down on her phone screen to see the 'sent' notification flash next to her message.

Same to you, T. Take care. Az Xox

Just as the train pulled in to the platform, Azalea turned off her phone notifications. The journey home was long enough, she didn't want to spend that time torturing herself over text messages she couldn't categorise in her head. She spent the next two hours thinking, contemplating what she should do for the rest of the evening. She needed to return to her sanctuary after such a long weekend of socialisation. She may have enjoyed it and made a friend, but no place in the world could compare to her king sized bed with her pumpkin orange blanket and mountain of pillows after a full day, never mind three. She'd missed the faint smell of dust on her paperback copies of books that rose beyond her reach until they hit the ceiling. She was almost a hoarder with how extensive her collection of books was; she read nearly everything she'd ever laid her fingers upon. Curling up for an evening, book in hand and with her cats warming her up, sounded like the perfect evening to return home to. Aside from the interrogation that was expected as soon as her big toe crossed the threshold, she had the full evening ahead of her. To eat junk. To read in the comfort of her room. To be by herself once more. Stepping off the train, she couldn't wait until that old oak door slammed behind her as she entered the door of her room. She just had to make it through the walk home and the questioning and then, finally, she could be herself again.

Whilst the walk from the train station to her home wasn't that far, it seemed longer every time she walked the path. Past the old oak that stood tall, splitting nearly into perfect halves from the weight of its towering branches. Past the fields of wheat, trampled and burnt by the local youths who spent their time mindlessly destroying the landscape and the hard work of the farming community. Just an hour down the road, either way, they could be in a city centre, but for some reason their chaos was limited to the small town they inhabited. Past the decrepit cottage, long since turned into a squat. It always felt weird to her, how close the countryside was to her house. A mere pebble thrown in any direction and she would hit a vacant plot of land, waiting to be upturned and used.

Walking the tiny trail, leading to her road, wild flowers sprouted from the gaps between paving stones. Daisies and buttercups, eager for the sun's glow to touch their delicate petals and leaves. She carefully tread, making sure she left the flowers intact. Nature's beauty was a thing to savour, not to demolish under heavy feet. Glancing up to the rooftops, she could see in the distance the smoke billowing from her own chimney top. Great, she sighed heavily. Her mother was waiting for her valiant return from fighting her own mind for a weekend. She probably had her lecture about self-worth, and working on making herself better, already memorised to heart just waiting for her arrival. She'd heard all the lectures and speeches to the point she could pick out the repetitive main quotes whilst half asleep. After a weekend of being open with her emotions, she just needed to shut down for a while. She didn't need to repeat the events of the freak show to a new audience. Step by step, she drew closer to her front door trying to conjure up an excuse to stop the initial bombardment. Tiredness from travelling? No, her mother would be able to tell she was wide awake. Period cramps? No, it was too early to be feeling them; she wasn't due on her cycle for another fortnight. Nausea was probably her best bet, due to her mother's inability to handle the smell of vomit. Nausea was her ticket to freedom. Grasping the handle to the front door, she took a deep breath. It was time to get the Q and A session over and done with.

Crying

A knot in my throat

My past on a platter

My dreams on ice

Feelings and emotions

Spouting from my lips with a lack of control

A progressive silence

An understanding nod

An urge to continue

But no words forming

Is this even helping?

Do I even care?

A look on our calendars

An agreed date

I'll be back once more

To unburden my load

One more counselling session

Can't hurt

Chapter 4

The interrogation didn't last as long as Azalea had thought it would. It was as if her mother had come prepared with a list of questions so she didn't have to think about anything other than the answers Azalea spouted. With every answer she gave, her mother would nod in agreement and listen eagerly to any of the answers that expanded from the initial 'yes' or 'no'. Her mother remained glued to the narration of the events as Azalea mentioned Tabby. She ignored just how much her heart raced at just the mention of her name.

"I'm glad you've found someone to talk to," her mother smiled cheerily as the stories came to a close. "I know it's hard for you."

Azalea shrugged. "It's not that hard, I just don't like it." As she sat across from her mother, her sweat sticking her to the leather settee, she focused her eyes on every little change around her. For years, the living room had hung dreamcatchers and chimes from the ceiling but in the last few months they had all disappeared one by one. The room became gloomier every time she sat in it. The once fiery red walls had been repainted a dull, life-sucking beige. The photo frames that littered the walls were now filled with landscapes of the sea and rivers instead of the funny face family portraits they used to contain. The coffee table was no longer coated in unopened mail or magazines with twig-like models on the front covers; it was bare aside from the four cork coasters that were placed neatly on the corners. The living room no longer felt like it was a space for the living. It seemed more like a set-up for a furniture catalogue, or the interior of a dolls' house a little girl had dedicated time to perfecting. Just sitting there reminded her why her own room had become her safe zone. The rest of the house felt it belonged to another family, not hers. She couldn't even remember the last time she had sat in a room with her mother for more than five minutes where they actually spoke to one another.

The room was so quiet you could hear a pin drop. They just sat there in complete silence, the only noise being the ticking of the kitchen clock in the background. For half an hour, they remained sat like that until, finally, Azalea had enough. Grabbing her stuff, she headed up the flight of stairs to her room, her cats following a few steps behind. She practically ran the few metres between her doorway and the top step. Opening her door, she took a deep breath. Scanning the room, she saw no noticeable changes, letting her exhale in relief. Her mother had got into the habit of moving things around whilst she was out of her room, so to see in untouched after a weekend she felt ecstatic.

Dropping her belongings by the side of the bed, she flopped backwards. How she'd missed her soft mattress. She was going to sleep like a baby that night. Closing her eyes, she felt the 8 fluffy paws hit the blanket seconds before the cats curled at either side of her. There was once a time when the cats didn't even come near her, back when Poppy was still around. They never used to be hers; she just inherited them when both she and the cats had no one else to turn to. For the last few months, they were always by her side whenever she was about to lose it. It was as if the cats sensed it before she even knew herself that she was being a wreck. She was so thankful.

Stretching, she fluttered her eyes open to see the cats mimicking her actions. She could still remember the days they'd been brought home as kittens, so tiny and mischievous. On Dali's first day, he'd managed to destroy Poppy's favourite t-shirt as he tried and failed to climb the washing basket. She had squealed for what felt like hours that she regretted bringing the little fellow home until he sleepily cuddled into her hip on the settee. Within that moment, it was obvious he had Poppy wrapped around his little paw. Storm was more behaved, even if she did like to perform disappearing tricks whenever it came to drying her off after she'd jumped in the bath with whoever was occupying it at the time.

Lying there on her bed, with Poppy's balls of fluff by her side, Azalea could no longer deny her mind of the thoughts. Every happy memory of Poppy came flooding in, as if the dam holding them back had finally eroded away. Fighting the urge to think of Poppy all the time was the only thing keeping her sane most days. It kept her from curling in bed all day in tears.

She'd never imagined she would one day be an only child, just like she never thought she would be how she was now. She'd always been the younger sibling, with an older sister to look up to for advice about clothes and make-up, amongst other things. If it weren't for Poppy, she would have been an entirely different person. More self-centred, or more spoiled. Having an older sister looking after her made her feel safe and protected. Nothing in the world could get to her because her big sister would always be there to fight for her. She'd do anything just to have her back, or to even get a goodbye.

Poppy's death still haunted the house. Even if her mother didn't say a word, Azalea could tell she still couldn't handle crossing the threshold into what used to be Poppy's room. Whilst it had been cleared to make way for a crafts studio for her mother, as well as a method by her mother to try to get her to open up about her feelings, the bare wooden floor gathered dust. Entering the room still felt too traumatic, too real, for the two of them. There were days in the past when Azalea had tried to convince Poppy to move out so she could have a bigger room alongside her own bathroom, but now she had to remind herself when she went to walk into her sister's room through the adjoining bathroom entrance that no one was on the other side.

Everything had happened so suddenly. She was so full of life, with so much to live for. But then, she was gone. Just like that. Like a cloud plucked from the sky, her existence was over. For days after her death, Azalea kept thinking she was trapped in a nightmare. She kept longing for her eyes to abruptly open, to end this world she couldn't believe in. When the days turned to weeks, the reality finally set in. Her best friend, the only person who truly understood her and her actions, was gone. No extra lives, no revivals, no restarts. Unlike the games she treasured and replayed a hundred times, death was permanent in the real world and nothing would change that.

When she finally stood by her sister's side again, it wasn't an elaborate storyline in a book created to bring the readers in, or a twist ending at the end of a film to give the audience hope that everything would be okay for the main characters. It wasn't the rebirth of the main character so he could defeat the villain for good, or a mythical ailment to preserve life forever. It was in the local funeral home after the police had released the body back to her mother. She lay on a cold metal tray, practically unrecognisable from her former self. Even looking for a millisecond was unbearable for Azalea. She lasted in the room for two minutes, most of which was spent looking at her mother. She'd always taken family deaths hard, but Azalea had never seen her mother react like this. Blank. Expressionless. Until that day, her mother had wept inconsolably but stood there, three weeks after her oldest daughter had become dead to the world, there was nothing on her face to indicate just what she was thinking. No tears, no anger, no defeat. She'd left the house in a skirt and blouse set for once instead of the usual paint-splattered, torn-in-places dungarees she spent most of her days in. Azalea couldn't remember the last time she'd seen her mother out of a dirty, inspiration-ready outfit.

It wasn't until after the funeral that Azalea noticed the real change in her mother. The fun-loving, tie-dyeing hippy that had lived inside her mother's soul had been killed and buried alongside Poppy. No longer did she enjoy her own freedom as an independent woman surrounded by young hearts to teach and treasure. Instead of thriving from and through her design work and crafts projects, Felicity 'Feather' Grace Hart finally got the first job that she'd define as "proper" in over a decade. With her managerial experience, she was picked up by an office in the city centre within a week of looking. When that job was set in stone, she retired her old moped Lilac to the scrapyard, exchanging the beautiful purple two wheeler she'd had since her own teen years for a suitable, reasonably priced car. The woman she had known and loved for her entire life transformed into a woman she'd never seen before in the space of six weeks. Curfews were added, counselling sessions became a part of regular life and fighting about them filled up the evenings before they went to their separate rooms to vent their frustrations.

Whilst Azalea still wished her mother was the light and free woman she used to be, she didn't regret all the changes. For years, her mother had believed in the benefits of natural sugars but finally, thanks to her long work schedule, she had finally forgotten her ban on all things unnaturally sugary. She used to have Poppy sneak in junk food for movie nights as her mother believed her sister wouldn't break the rules when it came to a healthy diet. They'd hide their bags of sweets behind the pillows or under the blankets for when their mother had been too drawn into the film to notice their actions. A nibble of a mars bar here, a crunch of a biscuit there. Whilst she was so focused, any snack was a-go. She missed the days of her mother's obliviousness, but at least now she didn't feel the urge to hide every chocolate bar away.

Awaking from her impromptu nap, Azalea found herself missing her other half once again. Reminiscing left an ache in her heart that she feared would never be fulfilled. Sitting up on the edge of her bed, she fumbled with getting her shoes on. She couldn't stay in this room when all she could think of was a short distance down the road. Grabbing her hoodie from the chair by the door, she thought of an excuse she could use on her mother for leaving the house. Her mother hated it when she randomly left the house without an explanation. As she ran down the stairs, she decided on what to say this time.

"I'm heading to the shops, I'll be back shortly!" She called to the front room, positive that's where her mother still lurked.

"Grab some milk!" She heard in response as the front door locked behind her. If her mother knew just where she was going, she'd be imprisoned for the rest of her living days. She wasn't supposed to go there alone. It had been forbade ever since her hospital stay. It was a general fear of the doctors and her mother that it could push her over the edge. She scoffed. It was one of the only places she felt she could be honest with herself. As her feet led the way, on a path they had taken many times in the last few months, she thought about what she would say today. She always felt the need to rehearse what to say prior with the limited time her excuses bought her. She knew what she said would make no difference either way, the response was always the same.

Heading through the cemetery gates, she walked down the centre towards the war memorial, trying to remember the fastest route to her destination. Plotting her course, she read the names aloud to herself as she passed. So many names of previous town occupiers she recognised from her visits. Walking carefully, avoiding the nettles that the cemetery caretaker clearly forgot to cut, she found the only headstone that truly mattered to her. Just looking at it reminded her of how much she had argued with her mother when they spent the afternoon picking it out. Her mother had insisted that the headstone have an engraving of a poppy next to her sister's details.

"It's what she would have wanted." She could hear her mother say, clear as day, as the sales representative led them around the yard where the examples stood. "She always loved poppies."

Before she could stop herself, she corrected her mother. "She hated poppies; they set off her allergies more than any other flower. She always thought it was dumb being named after something that made her nose itch and her eyes swell." Feeling like she needed to prove a point she moved from the headstone her mother's mind was set on. Walking to an example a few feet away she stopped. "This is the headstone she would want. Plain. Simple. Not too much fuss." Looking up she could see the annoyance in her mother's eyes. She knew that as soon as they were in the car there'd be another fight about Poppy's memorial. Her mother would argue about how she knew her daughter well enough to make decisions a mother should never have to make, whilst she would argue that Poppy wouldn't want such a big deal to be made. She was easy going; she wouldn't care if her resting place was under two twigs. They were fighting a lot, over the little details that made up the overall event. Azalea didn't even want to go, but it was apparently an important part of moving on according to her mother. They both needed this, and it had to be perfect. In the end, she gave in to her mother and let her pick the stupid headstone with a poppy on it.

In the centre of the headstone hung a photo plaque with Poppy's face gleaming from it. Even in picture form, just looking at her sister warmed Azalea's heart. This was the only place she still felt close to her. This is where her sister lay her head – in ashes form at least.

"Hey Poppy," she said feeling the cool of the wind hitting her cheeks already, "I miss you more than usual today. The cats have been helping, but it's hard to think about you without wanting to cry." She could feel her eyes welling up at just the mention of crying. She patted her jeans pocket, reminding herself she had tissues for when she inevitably starting crying in the exact spot she had cried many times before.

"Whilst I was away, I met someone you'd like." She murmured as she stared into her sister's lit up face. The picture was taken at the last party she attended before she passed. She was so excited to go out for the first time in months, she'd spent hours dolling herself up. Her mother had loved seeing her sister returning to her old self, so much so that she urged Poppy to pose for the picture Azalea was now looking at. It had only been taken a few weeks before Poppy's death but it already felt like it had been years since it happened. Her blue eyes were even more piercing than usual with the way she'd layered green and purple eyeshadow above her eyelids. It was hard to not be drawn in.

"She's weird, but who isn't these days? I think you'd get on with her, you seem quite alike." Thinking of Tabby felt weird whilst she sat talking to her sister, but she told Poppy everything, she didn't want her to miss out on anything happening in her life, even if it was only making friends. "The counselling session work itself was terrible, but it always has been. Bonding over shared experiences with other strangers? No thanks, I'd rather go back to my books and ignore the world for a day or two." As she examined her sister's headstone for any marks of dirt, or even worse bird shit, she noticed a spider running along the top of the stone. She leaned forward to blow it lightly off her headstone. If Poppy could see her headstone for just that second, she would have freaked out. Spiders were her equivalent of an arch nemesis. "I'm going to have to go now, before mum flips her shit too much at me being out too long. Just remember, I love you."

Azalea pulled herself to her feet and kissed her fingers before placing them on the top of the headstone. She'd do anything to go back to a time where Poppy would stumble into her room, drunken out of her mind, to give her a sloppy kiss and incredibly long hug before she headed to bed.

"Taken too soon." Azalea quoted her sister's headstone before turning to head home. There wasn't a truer statement in the world. Leaving the cemetery, she felt a hard, heavy breeze against the back of her neck. Pulling her hoodie tighter against herself, she headed to buy some milk to keep her mother unsuspicious.

Chapter 5

Behind the camera lens, Tabitha felt indestructible. Her doubts, her thoughts, her depression. When she had the camera in her fingertips, she felt like a completely different person, one without a trailer full of baggage dragging behind her.

"Smile," she urged, pointing the camera at Doris, the elderly woman across from her. For the longest time now, she'd spent her time shooting daily life in the care home when she visited, passing the good photographs over to the staff for if the families wanted copies or for the inevitable obituaries. Tabitha liked spending time with the people in the home. She basically grew up here when she visited her grandfather. This large family she could escape to every once in a while when living in foster care got hard. Most of the residents she knew and loved had passed from this place, either to more advanced care or to whatever they believed happened after death, but the few who remained still treated her like their own blood. She got birthday cards, Easter eggs, Christmas presents – the residents and care workers went above and beyond.

Doris chuckled, waving her hand in Tabitha's direction dismissively. "Go see your grandpa, kitten! I'm sure he'd love to see you!"

"Only once I see your glamorous smile!" As Doris giggled, she snapped a few more pictures, focusing on the happiness in her eyes. The part she always enjoyed the most was being able to capture the little moments that may be missed otherwise. That, plus not being the centre of attention made her want to get back into her photography professionally. It was too much of a risk though, to even have her name shared publicly again. Any bad memory from the past could reappear, and the main culprit always knew the worst of people to do his dirty work in his absence. He would have to be dead for her to even consider doing something she was passionate for instead of short-term jobs and cash-in-hand positions. She tried her best to avoid leaving any evidence she still existed.

"Tabby?" Nurse Ola approached, placing a cup of tea at the table for the woman. "I think I've just heard your grandad stirring, you ready to see him?"

Tabitha nodded, packing up her camera equipment swiftly. "I'll see you later," she smiled sweetly at Doris, winking in her direction.

As they approached her grandfather's room, she felt anxious. Would he even remember who she was this time, or even acknowledge her? The last time she came over to the care home, he just stared out his bedroom window for the hour she was there. She got it - he wasn't there like he used to be mentally, not anymore. She just wished that she had a chance to get to know him before the dementia hit. It was hard on her, knowing the only family member she knew didn't even remember who she was.

"He's been having a good time recently, you know," Ola encouraged her. "His short-term memory hasn't improved, but he is remembering some pieces of information and he has been able to communicate more with the other residents more than usual."

Tabitha smiled. It was always good to hear that things hadn't reached the worst point yet. She dreaded the day when she got the call to say that he was beyond the level of care that the care home could offer. As they walked, Ola gave her updates and stories about what had been going on since her last visit. It always comforted her, just how well the staff cared for everyone here. They treated them like they treated their own families, proudly sharing all the achievements they'd witnessed and Tabitha was always grateful for it. She felt like she never missed a moment with her grandfather with all the things she hears.

Ola patted her on her shoulder as she left her outside her grandfather's room. "Press the buzzer if you need us, remember? You don't have to do it all yourself."

"Thanks, Ola!" She called after her, her hesitation obvious. She could do this, she reassured herself. She had to.

Knocking on his door, she took a deep breath. Hopefully he was in a lucid state this time. Even if he didn't recognise her, as long as he was able to speak to her today it was better than nothing.

"Hello?" a low croak came from the room. Tabitha pushed herself and the door open. A quick scan of the room showed her grandfather, sat comfortably in his faux leather armchair by the window.

"Hey grandpa," Tabby smiled sadly in her direction. Sitting across from him on the matching footstool, she hoped he could at least recognise a bit of her.

Leaning forward and squeezing her hand, her grandfather smiled. "Cathy, I can't believe you've made it. Where's Tabby? Is she causing havoc with the staff again?" He glanced over his shoulder, a chuckle rumbling from his chest. "She's always been such an excitable 5 year old!" Standing up, he started rooting through his drawers frantically. "I'm sure I have a doll for her somewhere!"

Tabby sighed hard. She hated when he called her by her mother's name. It was one thing him not remembering her, it was another when he remembered her but didn't recognise her as the person in front of him.

"I'm Tabby, grandpa," she urged him to see her for her for once. Even if it was just for a moment, she wanted him to see her as Tabby, not as a stranger, not as her mother.

"Now, Cathy, don't fret – I'll find it," he dismissed her, completely ignoring the words that left her mouth. Every search of his belongings for the non-existent toy became more frenzied. With every door opening, he slammed it back, becoming more agitated.

"Grandpa, its okay," she pressed, hoping he would calm down. If he didn't, she'd need the nurses' assistance. When he lost his temper, it was a nightmare to try to control him. Looking his way, she could tell that nothing would relax him. Getting to her feet, she moved slowly towards the emergency button by the side of her grandfather's bed.

"For fuck sake!" He screamed, loud enough to wake the deaf woman in the room next door. Tabitha rushed and pressed the button hard as the lamp that was once on his side table next to his chair was shattered in thousands of pieces on the floor. As she rushed to his side to try and restrain him, a few other smashables met the same fate.

"Please, grandpa, stop," she pleaded just as the larger male nurses came bolting in. She backed away as the muscular nurses helped her grandfather back to her bed.

"Gerald, if you don't calm down you know we have to sedate you," one nurse firmly snapped in the direction of her grandfather as they help him down, "You know you can't just go around smashing everything."

"I don't care, I don't care, I DON'T CARE!" He shouted, anger forming in his eyes. "Where are my girls? I need my Tabby! Where's my tiny Tabby kitty cat? You've taken her haven't you? GIVE ME MY TABBY KITTY CAT!" With every word, his yells increased, decibel by decibel.

The nurses glanced at each other before throwing the look

Tabitha's way, all knowing they had no other choice. Pulling a capped needle from his breast pocket, he held her grandfather's arm looking for a usable vein. Taking the cap off, he poked the injection of Midazolam in releasing the chemical into his system. Tabitha couldn't watch as her grandfather fought initially before stopping completely.

The nurses looked at her sorrowfully. The worst part of it all was how this wasn't the first time and definitely wouldn't be the last time that her grandfather would need to be sedated during an outburst.

After visiting the care home, Tabitha head to the local coffee shop, fighting the urge to just wander into the closest bar for a smorgasbord of vodkas, rums and tequila. She just needed a drink in her hands, keeping her from her addictive nature. She sat, looking at all the generic artwork on the walls as her phone began to ping away to itself. Glancing at the screen, the messages kept appearing. Azalea, Laine, Laine, Laine, Laine, Laine.

You need to visit, Tabs, hate havin' cats for my only company and my mother may drive me insane. Az Xox

P.s. prepare for HUNDREDS of cat portraits. I may have taken a few… thousand.. :/ Az Xox

Chuckling herself, glad for the distraction and happy her new friend still wanted to speak to her, she typed quickly back.

Sort a date with your mum, and I'll be over ASAP once I've sorted it with work. T x

She skimmed Laine's short messages quickly. That boy was eager, and she wasn't sure whether she should be flattered or scared.

So, T, I think we should go out. L x

Only if you want to. L x

Sorry if I'm being pushing about it, you're just so cute. L x

Sorry, I'll stop texting now. L x

You're honestly gorgeous, T. L x

She couldn't help the little smirk that escaped her. It had been a long time before anyone had called her cute, nevermind gorgeous. He wasn't a bad piece of eye candy either.

Don't stop texting. Flatter me some more ;) T x

She could feel herself blushing. She couldn't even remember the last time she'd flirted with anyone, especially someone as good-looking as Laine. She knew she had to take the chance as it presented itself, even if it went nowhere. It was time for her to move on with her life. Her past was behind her and not moving forward made it seem like she had just stood still after it all.

Don't want to risk you getting big-headed now ;) Fancy meeting Saturday? L x

No pressure. L x

Her blush grew. She'd be an idiot not to go. How could she tell her friend it would all be okay and that she would be able to work through it all if she couldn't? She had to take the leap back out there and be more careful this time around. No falling too hard for the bad guy, or being a piece of spoiled meat to hungry animals.

It's a date ;) T x

That Saturday, she spent hours in front of the mirror preening. She felt like a proper teenager for once. She never had the chance before. She'd never been on a proper date. Looking in the mirror, she looked like someone else. Someone who deserved happiness. She just hoped that after everything she had been through, she was still able to be happy after all the time that had passed. All she wanted was to be with someone who made her smile and laugh, like Azalea had. With one last glance of the beautiful woman in the mirror, Tabitha set off to meet the man who could possibly change her opinion of men for good.

Chapter 6

It had been nearly two months since they'd last seen each other in person, but Azalea and Tabby's relationship just kept growing. They spoke on the phone near enough every day, as well as various text messages and video calls. It was nice, Azalea thought, to have someone you could speak to no matter what. Within a few days, Tabby would be landing in Azalea's little village, prepared to run amuck in the countryside. Thankfully her mother hadn't fully interrogated her about Tabby's visit. She didn't ask how long she was staying, what was planned or how well she knew this girl. The lack of questions reminded her slightly of how easy-going her mother used to be, but she knew she wasn't returning to her old ways. Her mother just didn't want her to lose the only friend she truly had anymore.

Preparing the inflatable bed on the floor, Azalea felt slightly guilty. She knew there was still a perfectly good mattress in Poppy's old room but she couldn't face opening that door and dragging her sister's mattress across the hallway. In her mind, it still belonged to Poppy and no one else could use it. She shrugged. Tabby could just take her bed. She was content sleeping on the inflatable, just as long as the cats were kept at bay. More than one inflatable guest bed had been lost to their claws in the past, and she wasn't going to risk another one.

Azalea was so excited, knowing her best friend was going to be present in her real world in a matter of days. She could feel her brain keeping track of the passing hours, ticking until Tabby was by her side again. Her heart still raced every moment she crossed her mind. She couldn't wait to show her around her quaint little village, with its' hooligans and neighbourhood watch. "I've never been to the countryside before," she remembered Tabby saying on the camping trip as they stayed up late around the fire, "I've never really even left the city." She hoped Tabby would enjoy herself when she stayed; she wanted her to come and visit more than once.

Azalea rushed to straighten up her entire living space with anticipation. She couldn't remember the last time she had friends stay over. It was easily over a decade ago. She never really felt close enough to anyone to open up her private area to them. Tabby was different though. She felt like Tabby would get it. She would understand why she is the way she is. She'd take all of Azalea's weird behaviours and tendencies in stride. That's what friends were supposed to do - to accept each other inside and out.

Having a real friend was a first for Azalea. Throughout her younger days, she always sought companionship with Poppy. She never felt that she'd need anyone else in her life. Even in school, she was usually that one weird child no-one had the time to talk to, but that was the way she preferred it. When she was alone, she could let her mind wander. She didn't have to listen out for what other people around her were saying in conversations, or pay attention to the real world. She could slip into her dream world where everything was safe and perfect. Whilst other children were playing tag, she was imagining she was from another planet, waiting for the mothership to take her back home. Her insecurities left her alone, but as she grew she seemed to mind less. She never thought she'd need another friend with Poppy by her side but now she was truly alone and hoping Tabby could at least slightly fill the hole her sister left.

Waiting at the train station, Azalea paced by the arrivals board. Her local station may have been small but she wanted to make sure she couldn't be missed the second Tabby emerged from her platform. The tapping of her feet on the tiles as she paced was filling her with ease as the rest of her body shook with anxiety. She was supposed to be here by now. It had already been delayed by a half hour thanks to bad winds, but the train was due to arrive around ten minutes ago. Azalea could barely remain patient.

"Stay calm for Tabby," she sighed to herself, knowing Tabby would be here as soon as she could. She just had to keep her anxiety at bay. As she stared at the main arriving platform, she could hear the sound of a train approaching. Her smile spread happily across her face. It was here. Finally. She practically ran to the platform, nearly falling head over heels in the process. As she saw Tabby, her luggage in tow, her heart flipped inside her ribcage. There she was, ready for the week ahead of them both.

As Tabby made her way to Azalea's side, Azalea couldn't help but notice the grin that spread across her perfect lips and the giddiness in her step. She was glad she wasn't the only one feeling that way. "Hello stranger," Tabby's voice purred as she reached Azalea. "Have you missed me much?"

Azalea chuckled. "Only as much as you've missed me."

"Oh, so more than anything then!" Tabby exclaimed, the smile on her face growing larger. As if by instinct, she went to pull Azalea into a hug before hesitating. Not wanting to reject her new best friend, Azalea closed the gap and wrapped her arms around Tabby's shoulders. She'd grown to the idea of letting some people touching her since they'd last seen each other, which surprised her mother dearly. She'd almost forgotten the routine she used to have of giving her mother a goodnight kiss and hug before she scampered off to bed. But now it was back, and it seemed to thrill her mother that she was taking another step in the right direction.

"The counselling is paying off!" She could almost hear her mother's voice chime in her mind. Azalea knew her ability to hug her family again wasn't down to the work of counsellors, but to Tabby's insistence. The girl thrived off hugging and she used it to express more emotions than a normal person could imagine. If Tabby insisted, Azalea would hug her every single time. She didn't want to make this girl, willing to spend time with her, feel awkward or uncomfortable.

Walking, practically on clouds, Azalea led the way as Tabby trailed behind with her suitcase in tow. With every step, she pointed out a landmark to Tabby making sure she took it all in. She could hear the fascination in Tabby's voice as she gazed at the countryside and its beauty.

"Have you been up to much?" Tabby queried as her feet fell in sync with Azalea's steps. Had she? The months had flown by without much notice and she kept doing the same things she did to begin with. College work. Looking for a job. Sitting and reading for hours on end, dvds at the ready for if the books ever began to bore her which they rarely did.

The Summer sun glared down on the pair as they continued walking. She shrugged. "Just the usual amount of nonsensical bullshit to fill the passing of time. How about you?"

A glimmer of happiness appeared in the corner of Tabby's eye as Azalea glanced at her. "Do you remember the guy from the campsite, the one with the lack of common sense?"

The memory of Laine nearly stumbling into her naked self-flooded her mind in an instant. "Yeah. What about him?" Azalea knew just what she was going to say before she'd even responded and she could almost feel her envy projecting out of her flesh.

"Let's just say he is a nice guy and I hope to be seeing more of him," she smiled coyly, winking in her direction.

"Of course," she thought to herself in annoyance as she tried to think of a reasonable response to Tabby. "He was a handsome guy; of course Tabby would fall for him. Just like any sane woman would."

"Good luck with that," she responded smiling half-heartedly. "Other than being a bit of an idiot, he didn't seem too bad." After that, the subject of Laine and men in general was dropped for the remainder of their walk. Azalea didn't want to approach the subject any more than necessary. Men were just not something on her mind.

Upon the front door swinging open, Azalea's mother pounced like a starving lioness finding her first wandering wildebeest calf. "You must be Tabitha," she mused, "Azalea has said so much about you. I'm Miss Hart but you can call me Felicity if you'd like." She held out her hand for a handshake in Tabby's direction, curious to see if she would take it or if she suffered the inability of touch Azalea had suffered for months.

"The pleasure is all mine," Tabby purred, ignoring Felicity's hand and swooped in for a friendly hug, "Az has told me only great things about you." Azalea smirked as she caught the look of shock in her mother's face as Tabby finally let her go. She could tell her mother was expecting nothing more than a handshake, never mind a full blown hug from a stranger she had never met before.

It didn't surprise Azalea that Tabby was good with parents after the many hours she'd spent reminiscing about the few things she remembered about her own. The night time stories, the family picnics in the park, the days out as a perfect unit. It made Azalea almost wish she had two functional parents instead of an absent father and irregular mother. She didn't mind not growing up having a father in her life, truth be told, but part of her always wished her childhood was more common so others could relate to her situation. Not many people around her aside from her sister knew how it felt to be raised by a hippy who believed the world was full of wonder instead of devastation.

Taking Tabby's belongings, and leading the way in the process, Azalea led Tabby to her room. Tabby halted for a second at the entrance as she admired Azalea's room. Just having someone in her personal space made Azalea feel embarrassed, her cheeks flushing crimson. The bland walls were coated with film posters, display towers and photographs. Most of the cream carpet bordering the towers was covered with scattered piles of DVDs and books. It was hard to find a home for everything when she had a particular order for putting things away – by genre and then alphabetically. Most of her things fit into a few sections, so she was constantly reworking her shelves. Her laptop took up a majority of her bedside table, her camera tucked below it on the shelf, the rest of the table covered in small posed figures from a multitude of animes, games and films.

"I'm a bit of a collector," she said aloud as nonchalantly as she could muster. She didn't like the idea of being judged on all of the little parts that made her. She'd collected everything she found cute or cool since she was a child. Any figurines that stood out to her, or any DVDs that she thought sounded perfect for her ever-growing set. If she opened both of her cupboard doors at once, she'd be sucked into an avalanche of plushies. Placing Tabby's belongings by the side of the bed, she took a seat, looking at the girl whose opinion mattered more than anything.

"I like it," Tabby smiled, "It's just so you." A thicker blush hit Azalea's cheeks. She shook her hair to cover her face. "So," Tabby continued, as she attempted to make eye contact with Azalea, "What do you want to do first?" She walked over to Azalea's side and sat beside her.

Azalea contemplated the possibilities – there was so much they could do. "You can decide," she shrugged, "You're my guest after all."

Chapter 7

As the night fell, the moon shimmering through her bedroom window, the girls lay down on the bed for a moment, both sets of eyes closed to the world. After an afternoon of eating junk food curled in blanket cocoons in front of the television with terrible horror films, at the request of Tabby who'd had enough of the sun after her train journey, they decided it was time to have a typical girly sleepover, with secrets and makeovers. Firstly, though, they needed to gather their energy for the night ahead with a short rest. The cats had kept them company for a while but disappeared as soon as they heard the tear of a sachet. They loved Azalea, but not as much as they loved food.

Pushing herself up after a minute or so, Azalea looked towards Tabby. She looked so peaceful just lay there perfectly still. Her pale skin stood out so much compared to the pumpkin-coloured bedsheet that covered the double bed; she was practically florescent. Her bleached hair spread across the space between the pair. Azalea held back the urge to reach out and stroke it. She pushed her own hair behind her ear instead to keep her fidgety fingers busy.

As if she felt the not-so-secret glances, Tabby opened her eyes and smirked at Azalea. "What are you looking at?" she purred, tightly turning her lips into a faked pout. "Do I have something on my face or am I just grotesque?"

"No," Azalea smirked back, "You'd never be counted as grotesque anyway, supermodel. Have you seen you in a mirror?" Moving towards the edge of the bed, further away from Tabby, she placed her feet on the floor kicking the inflatable bed in the process. "I was just waiting for you to join reality again and stop daydreaming." Pulling herself to her feet, she moved towards her chest of drawers, barely noticeable between her tower units completely stuffed with figures and models with costumes and props hanging off the corners. Bending over to reach the bottom drawer, Azalea swiftly turned to face the door. Though the door was shut, she still wanted to make sure her mother didn't suddenly appear and discover her hiding place. As she bent further, pulling the drawer out of its frame, a small chink of glass hitting something hard echoed around the room. As she reached in to retrieve the bottle of rum she'd hidden one day whilst her mother was at work, she felt a cold slither of metal against her hand. Her hand grasping the neck of the bottle, she yanked her hand free of the hidden compartment before her brain told her to fish out the other hidden objects too. Before she placed the drawer back in position, Azalea flung the bottle to the safety of her bed, landing at Tabby's side.

As she looked at the bottle, Tabby's original grin turned into an expression Azalea had never seen on her before. It was as if she had been knocked nauseous by the mere sight of the alcohol. Concerned, Azalea took the bottle from the bed and placed it aside, out of Tabby's view. "Are you okay?" Almost out of habit from her times with an upset older sister, Azalea took Tabby's hand in hers and squeezed. "If you're not a drinker, or have issues with it, I can put it away. I just thought it might be nice to toast a fun week to come."

Tabby shook her head, her lips parting and pursing for a few seconds as she contemplated her words, Azalea looking at her. "No, I'm fine. I just have bad memories of that rum is all. If you've got anything else hidden anywhere, Smuggler Barbie, I'd happily take a swig to celebrate."

"I've got nothing at hand, unfortunately. The rum was the only thing I was able to smuggle that my mother would never notice. It was hidden in my sister's room and I grabbed it before she knew it even existed." Over the few months since they'd met, Azalea had made it a habit to not discuss Poppy more than necessary. Poppy's story was always better heard in person instead of over the phone or by text. In person, she could see how Tabby truly reacted to the news. There had already been so many people who acted like it was an atrocity before acting completely indifferent when they were face to face. She wasn't looking for comfort from strangers, just basic understanding. Poppy still had so much life to live, but they acted as if she was an old dog and her death was inevitable.

"Az..." Tabby whispered, nearly inaudibly, "If you want to talk about what happened to her, I'm always here. I'm not going anywhere." Azalea faintly smiled. Sighing deeply, she knew it was time to discuss Poppy.

"It all started when..." she faced Tabby and took a deep breath. It had been so long since she'd discussed her sister's demise, she was unsure if she could get through the entire story without bursting into tears and curling into the foetal position. "It started when Poppy met Hunter. He's the reason she's dead. He murdered her in cold blood, and there's nothing I can do to bring her back." The flood of tears started then, coating her cheeks as they dripped off her face.

Before she could continue, she felt a finger wiping away her tears. "Hush, Az. It's okay. We'll talk about this when you're ready." Tabby pressed her lips lightly on Azalea's cheek and kissed the tears away. "I'm not going anywhere, so you've got eternity to tell me." Pulling Azalea into her chest as the tears carried on streaming, Tabby stroked her hair gently away from her face. Humming lightly, her arms wrapped around Azalea's body, squeezing her tightly. She remained perfectly still as Azalea shook with her practically inaudible cries. Not knowing what else to do, Tabby brought Azalea closer to herself, her face buried in Azalea's head, her lips resting inches away from her forehead. "Remember to breathe, sweetheart." Tabby whispered into the air, "I need you here."

Azalea opened her eyes wide, a yawn escaping her throat. Looking to her side, she found Tabby, arms still tucked around her body, oblivious to the world in her sleep state. A smile snuck onto her lips as she detached herself from her friend. Stretching, she couldn't believe last night. She hadn't cried like that in so long and in an instant of mentioning what happened to Poppy, not even in great detail, the floodgates opened. She shook her head, thinking of the night before all over again. Tabby didn't seem to have minded her reaction. She made her feel like she was safe to discuss whatever she wanted at her own pace. It wasn't like it had been with the rest of the world. As soon as most people found out her sister had been murdered, they wanted every single detail straight away, no matter how much it hurt to talk about. It was as if the story was more important than the life lost.

Looking back over Tabby as she slept, Azalea was glad she was here. She wanted to be honest with her and she was prepared to discuss her sister more. The subject of Poppy had felt taboo for the last eight months. Even with the counsellors, she could barely discuss her. She focused more on her emotions than the actual circumstances of her sister's death. She wanted to be able to remember Poppy without feeling the hole in her heart grow further. Tabby was the perfect person to discuss her with, though it was going to take some time to get the full story out if her reaction the previous night was anything to go off. It didn't matter. As long as the full story was shared and finally off her chest, she might feel better, or at least have someone who would understand her better.

Leaning over Tabby in search of her slippers by the side of the bed, she felt a sudden grasp on her wrist. She looked at Tabby to see her eyes wide open. "Sorry," Tabby whispered, "force of habit." Pushing herself up by her elbows, she smiled tiredly in Azalea's direction. Staring into Azalea's eyes, she queried "How are you faring?"

Azalea shrugged. "I guess I'm not ready to tell you the full story just yet. I thought I was but," she paused for a moment, looking back at Tabby, her heart beating frantically as she contemplating telling her more, "I just don't think I'm ready to remember it all again." Sitting up on her bed, forgetting about the slippers entirely, she could feel her lungs heavy in her chest. "It ruined me, you know? It's why I've always hated counselling, I don't want to go back to the worst moment of my life repeatedly! That's just asking for a bad time."

Nodding in response, there was a silence before Tabby responded. Of course she understood, Azalea thought, she was in the same position. No one goes to counselling because their life is all dandy. "Well, either way, whenever you are ready – I'm ready." Tabby sat up and reached for Azalea's hand. Taking it in hers, she laced their fingers together and squeezed reassuringly. Azalea squeezed back as Tabby raised the hands to her lips and lightly kissed the back of Azalea's hand. "And maybe one day, I'll tell you my deep dark secrets too."

"I bet you will," Azalea half-heartedly smiled, "I'm sorry I'm a mess. Remembering Poppy and Hunter and everything else just drains the life out of me." Azalea loosened her hand from Tabby's grip and readjusted her pose, tucking her legs beneath her bottom with her thighs pressed side by side. A silence hung in the air for a while as they just looked at each other from across the bedspread, an indecision lingering in the air. There was no need for words. Both wished to press the other for more details, more titbits of their autobiographies never previously seen, but they knew that it wasn't right. As much as Azalea wished to know about Tabby and her life, she knew that pushing for answers would ultimately push her friend away.

After too long of a silence for her liking, Azalea rose, pulling Tabby alongside her. "I want to take you on an adventure today," she smirked at her friend, "Somewhere I've never shown anyone before. Get ready for the best day of your life!" Quickly changing, the pair prepared for their outing. Sunscreen and bug repellent coating their skin. Bags packed to the zips with treats, drinks and necessities. They headed for the door, rucksacks flung over their shoulders.

Shutting the front door behind her with a loud thud, calling goodbyes to her mother abruptly, Azalea took Tabby's hand and led the way. Glancing at Tabby regularly, Azalea could see the excitement in her eyes. Her inner butterflies fluttered, filling her with a wave of anxiety that dawdled. They walked, sun high above them in the sky lightly glazed by plump white clouds, feeling the heat on their bodies as their feet continued plodding their steps. Step by step, Tabby followed Azalea as she headed towards a thick, wooded area. "It's not far," Azalea smiled, "And honestly it is spectacular." Weaving through the thick brush, Azalea's feet found her hidden path. Practically skipping, she pulled Tabby alongside her, knowing she was nearly there. As the clearing opened up in front of the pair, her feet came to a final stop.

Tabby's jaw dropped as Azalea finally let go of her hand. Removing her rucksack from her shoulders, Tabby scanned the view around her in complete awe. The clearing sat at the top of a hill, with the glorious British countryside spread in front of her. There were fields for miles, as far as her eyes could see, with trees lining where the plots of lands separated, no fences ruining the landscape. Bushes and shrubbery laced the spots where trees did not. At the bottom of the hill, a path and stream ran along the side of each other, the path twisting as the river did almost as if it was as natural as the river itself. Small country homes were scattered and scarce in the area, with small clusters of smoke coming from their chimneys. "It's so beautiful," Tabby murmured. Her voice was so soft it was almost missed as the wind blew.

"I thought you'd like it," Azalea smiled deeply; "I've always loved it here." Opening her rucksack, she unfolded a blanket and placed it in the centre of the clearing, lay as smoothly as possible. As Tabby pulled her professional camera out of her rucksack to take some pictures of the wonderful landscape, Azalea took out a portable speaker from her own. Hooking it up to her phone, a light beat started to echo in the clearing. The music became clearer and it was as if it had captured the pair in an impenetrable bubble.

As the sweet sounds of the Les Miserables soundtrack filled the clearing, Azalea closed her eyes. The clearing had always felt safe to her and now here she was, sharing her sacred space with a girl she trusted impeccably. She hadn't even shown Poppy the clearing, even though she discovered it whilst thinking of her. Poppy had been gone for the weekend when she'd found the clearing. She was off with Hunter, doing whatever they spent their alone time doing.

She was a jealous teenager back then. A stubborn fifteen year old girl who missed having her best friend by her side, the situation made even worse by her crush on her sister's boyfriend. Poppy was in love though. She knew it was going to happen eventually, losing her sister to a man but she hadn't expected it to happen when it did. Poppy was seventeen when she met him – Hunter Marshall.

He was the typical pretty, bad boy every girl thought they could change. Dark brown hair with chocolate eyes. A stubborn look of annoyance constantly plastering his face. A bit of a temper, but never really threatening. A muscular chest that could make an Adonis envious. A teasing smirk that women lost their minds over and hearts to. He rarely smiled, but when he did she could almost hear every woman in close proximity swooning. His laugh was so perfect, it could dazzle anyone. Poppy was head over heels and Azalea was close behind her.

Azalea kept her crush quiet, not wanting to ruin her relationship with Poppy over an unrequited hormone-induced love affair that only existed in her mind. Back when they were both lustfully aching over Hunter, neither of the sisters could see him as the bad person who he was inside. It killed Azalea knowing that they'd never seen it coming.

Even though Poppy had never stood in the clearing, Azalea felt a longing for her sister being sat there thinking of her. She wished she could have shared the spot with her, that they'd had a chance to be sat there just like she was now. Looking up, Azalea could see Tabby still snapping away happily to herself. She quickly wiped a lingering tear out of her tear duct and smiled in Tabby's direction. She may not have had a chance to show her sister her special spot, but at least she had shared it with someone who could enjoy it as much as she knew Poppy would have.

Tabby took a final photo of the clearing and joined Azalea on the blanket on the ground. The music filled their silence with its soothing notes. Taking Azalea's hand in her own, Tabby squeezed gently. "Thank you for bringing me to your secret lair. I know it means a lot." Azalea smiled back towards Tabby before staring out into the countryside ahead of her.

"This place has always made me feel safe. I feel like I can be myself without people seeing me as the dead girl's sister, or a victim. It's like a hideaway from the real world."

"It's honestly making me feel the same." Tabby smiled with a sadness in her eyes. "I want to tell you something and I think now is the best time to do it." She held her breathe for a moment, as if she was deciding whether to continue.

"You can tell me anything," Azalea looked deeply into the eyes of the girl who had always seemed so brave as the tears loomed in her eyes. "I promise."

"I know," Tabby nodded, taking a deep breath. "Just please, don't react like everyone else."

Unsure of how to respond, Azalea watched as Tabby yanked roughly at her hair. In an instant, every hair that had hung on Azalea's head was clumped together in her fists. She placed the hair at her side and let out a sigh. Glancing up to Azalea, Tabby felt nervous and embarrassed. "Well?" She questioned as her eyes met Azalea's.

I feel naked

Revealing myself to you

As if you're judging

Every fault

Every mark

Every flaw

On full display

I feel bare to the world

And for once

I am not hiding

I am not embarrassed

I am just me

Chapter 8

Sat in the awkward silence, Azalea couldn't think of how to respond. It has merely been a minute since Tabby revealed her scarred scalp but to the pair it might as well have been a thousand years. Tabby kept her eyes focused on the blanket, eyes blinking back the tears. "How?" is all Azalea's throat appeared to be able to muster. Taking Tabby's hand in her own, she stroked her thumb along the side of her index finger soothingly.

One more deep breath and Tabby was ready to speak. Her eyes remained glued to the ground as she spoke, but it was understandable. "Two years ago, I was in a very bad place. I was constantly high, or drunk, or doped up on something or other. The guy I was with – Olly – was a piece of scummy shit. When I was finally ready to leave, bags packed, sober enough to realise just how I needed out of that place, he caused this as a parting gift." She gestured to her scalp, the only part of her skin with any colour showing. Whilst the rest of her flesh was as pale as snow, the scar tissue appeared to be a faint crimson.

A laugh briefly escaped her lips as she glanced up to see Azalea's reaction – she still seemed to be in complete shock at the situation at hand. "I know, it's horrendous. Hence the wig. It healed, but the follicles were so damaged that I could never grow hair again. I tried being bald for about a week, but the stares..."

she hesitated before continuing, as if she remembered how bad the reactions were, "The stares made it unbearable. The wigs might irritate my scalp but at least I don't have strangers gawking at me constantly."

Azalea shook her head. "It's not the worst I've seen, and I doubt it ever will be." She turned her right palm to face Tabby, her scar twisting with the motion. "We've both been scarred and have to live with it, but you shouldn't need to hide it away."

Tabby scoffed. "Says little miss contact lenses! You hide your eyes away from the world, you'd never cope with any scars that make people recoil in fear!" Anger heated up in Azalea's chest. She hadn't felt that she'd been hiding away. She felt like she was protecting herself more than anything. She shoved Tabby's hand back at her as she rose to her feet. Turned away, one by one, she removed her contacts before turning once more to face Tabby. As Tabby focused on Azalea's blind eye, it was obvious she regretted her words.

"I didn't know..." Tabby looked away, the regret hanging over her. "I'm so sorry, Az." Azalea shrugged; there wasn't much to say to the matter. The words were out there. They couldn't be taken back as hard as they tried. "I...I thought you just hated your eye... your eye colour or something." She stuttered. "I didn't realise..." She stopped talking, as if she wanted to prevent digging herself deeper into a hole she couldn't crawl out of.

"It's fine," Azalea shrugged again, "The damage is done. I shouldn't have reacted how I did either. I just didn't expect that. Your hair looked so real, so it was creepy to see it just be yanked from your scalp!"

"Hair glue," Tabby smirked, the air becoming easier to breathe. "And it's a human hair wig. Expensive to buy and hard to maintain, but it was more believable. That and the synthetic ones gave me more of an itch."

It felt awkward, Azalea thought in her head, to be able to discuss their damage so easily aloud. It had taken months before Azalea could even write her issues down, the journal being another suggestion her mother found online for coping with mental health issues. Apparently being open with you, even if it is just in writing, is better than keeping it in – or so some counsellors encouraged.

"I'm sorry to be so blunt about it," Tabby continued, "I felt like by the end of the week the glue wouldn't keep so you'd figure it out on your own. I just wanted to be the one to tell you my damage, not gravity."

"Your bluntness makes you who you are," Azalea shrugged in Tabby's direction, debating if it was worth putting the lenses back in her eyes. Flicking them aside, she decided against it. She hated the feel of them anyway and at this very second in her sacred place, she didn't need to hide away who she was. "And at least you were ready to be honest. I might never have told you about my eye otherwise. It's not exactly my best quality."

"And clearly, my hair is mine," Tabby smirked placing her wig in her bag with the rest of her treasured possessions. "I still feel like a bit of a freak without it on, but if you're going to brave here without your lenses I can't complain now, can I?" As the playlist changed, now softer than before as the breeze started to pick up through the trees, Tabby's eyes led her to the horizon. Staring out into the distance, the thump of the music occasionally interrupting her trail of thought, a whimper could be heard.

"Tabby, you're not a freak and you know it. There's nothing wrong with you! You're gorgeous, with a complexion to die for and a body every girl envies you for. You're beautiful, don't doubt yourself."

"Bullshit," Tabby scoffed, moving her gaze to her feet. "I've never been beautiful and I never will be." She sighed, shaking her head. "You don't need to lie to me about my looks; I know I'll never be a model looking like this." She scratched her nails along her jeans, trying to distract herself from the topic in any way.

Glancing at the girl she found more beautiful than a thousand unique sun rises, Azalea told her head to overcome her doubts and to act like she needed to. Azalea walked back towards Tabby, arms outstretched. Pulling Tabby up without any further words, she leaned in and kissed her on the lips lightly. Gently at first, but within seconds a passion flared inside her she could not extinguish. She pressed harder as Tabby's mouth responded, urging her on. Pulling her in tighter to her chest, a smile formed on Azalea's lips. As she pulled her face away from Tabby to get a breath of air, she caught the shimmer of the tears running down Tabby's cheek. Azalea wiped it away hesitantly before stepping back.

"You are the most beautiful person I have ever met, Tabitha Dixon, and I doubt I will ever meet anyone I find more beautiful in this world. You're amazing, inside and out. Ignore your head, it's lying to you."

A look of confusion remained plastered on Tabby's face. She stared into Azalea's eyes, questioning what had just happened;

unsure of what words could be used to describe the situation. Azalea stared right back, focused on Tabby's reaction. She'd overwhelmed herself by kissing Tabby, so she couldn't imagine what was going on inside Tabby's head. She was an idiot. She should have never made a move like that. Tabby was her friend, with no interest in her in that way. She had a sort-of boyfriend and clearly swung for that team. She couldn't comprehend her own feelings in her mind. She saw Tabby as a friend, someone to trust, and someone she could never lose. She didn't see her as her girlfriend, or anything along those lines – why had she kissed her? She cursed herself, her brain thinking of every swear word that summed up her idiocy. They all described her in that moment. As much as her body urged her to kiss Tabby, she should have ignored the loins and listened to her head. The regret lingered in her heart, knowing she could never take her actions back. She'd never forget it, and she doubted Tabby would.

Shaking her head, as if to forget exactly the moment that sprung the silence they currently faced, Azalea roughly packed away her possessions into her rucksack, pulling it swiftly onto her shoulders. Tabby sprang back to life, mimicking Azalea's actions. With both of their bags packed and ready to go, the pair remained silent as they left the clearing in the shadows.

Heading back home, Azalea didn't know what to say. Should she apologise? She was as surprised as Tabby for her own actions. If she could take it back, she would in an instant. Tabby's muteness persisted, pacing her steps to remain in sync with Azalea's though she kept a distance. Was she scared? Was this all a delayed reaction? Every part of her ached for a noise from Tabby. Even if it was indirect. A sneeze, a cough, a sniffle. Anything to prove that she was still there and not just a figment of her imagination.

How insane was she, to think something like that would be okay? She glanced in Tabby's direction. Her lips remained stuck together, as if they were frozen, and her eyes stared ahead without blinking. She'd give anything to see what she was thinking at that moment, just to see if Tabby was okay. To make sure she wasn't hated.

As they hit the path leading back to her home, Azalea felt a hand slither into her own. With a light squeeze, Tabby's hand held tightly to hers. As she peered out the corner of her vision, she could see Tabby smiling at her. Though the smile did not quite reach Tabby's eyes, Azalea felt her own lips respond. A second later, she was pulled into Tabby's grasps, where she hugged her in a dead man's grip. "I'm sorry," she could hear Tabby whisper.

"You have nothing to be sorry for, Tabs." She squeezed her friend fiercely back. "I'm the sorry person here." She patted Tabby on the shoulder and pulled away. Once again Tabby took her hand and she held it as they walked the remainder of the steps to her home.

Chapter 9

Before the pair knew it, the second day of Tabby's visit had flown by, as if time sped up just to irritate them. They'd spent the rest of their afternoon filled with small talk and enjoying each other's company. The actions of their little hike had long been forgotten, or as far away from their thoughts as it could be. Urging Tabby to take the bed, Azalea found herself getting all curled in her blankets on the pumped-up mattress, content in her life for the first time in what felt like an eternity.

The nightmares came back again that night. She'd saw it all over again, as if she had it stuck on a loop. The blood. The gore. For years before, Horror had been a big part of her life. Bingeing horror was her evening activity, with a mountain of sweets to share with her sister. She didn't need its' gore anymore. She'd lived it.

She was stood back at her front door once more, swung slightly ajar, with only flickering light coming from within. The bowl of candy was kicked onto the pavement, with the remnants of pumpkin splashed up the exterior stonework. She didn't want to go in, but she knew she had no choice – she never did. The screams got louder with every step she took forward. She ached for her feet to carry her backwards, or for her body to consent to turning around and fleeing. As she pushed the open door further, she was confronted with the blood splattered across the carpets.

Where it seeped into the fabric, it squished below her feet. She continued slowly, preparing herself for the sight before her. Heading into the living room, she was confronted by him. Hunter stood there, kitchen knife in hand already stained with crimson, a grimace plastered over his face. Lay behind his feet was Poppy, painted head to toe in her own fluids. As dead as she looked, Poppy's chest still rose up and down with a light splutter coming from between her lips. Her eyes flicked open to catch Azalea's. "Run," Poppy mouthed, pleading with her sister. She already knew she couldn't. This part of the scene was wrong. The amount of times she'd replayed the scene in her mind must have altered her memory. Poppy wasn't meant to be on the floor already. She was meant to be sat up, Hunter behind her, knife lightly grazing her flesh as he moved it up and down.

She closed her eyes for a mere moment, and there she was. Where she was really when Poppy was on the ground. Where she remained when Poppy needed her the most. Tossed aside at the other side of the room, a hole formed in the back of her skull. Relatively deep, but not enough to kill her. She could only see out of the one eye now, the other bled too profusely to see anything from. Trying to pull herself up, the dizziness defeated her, leaving her to watch the murder once again. She could hear Poppy pleading, whispering frantically at Hunter. The pleas did nothing. With one final thrust of his knife, Poppy was gone. She frantically gripped her mobile in her pocket, hoping help was on the way, before the blackness finally conquered her.

As Azalea shot up in the pitch darkness, the images remained painted to her eyelids. She couldn't forget Poppy, lay lifeless in front of her whilst she did nothing. She should have done something, anything, for Poppy. Her own life wasn't as important as Poppy's was. She had a future ahead of her, a full life's plan. Azalea had nothing of the sort. The grim reaper should have kept at bay instead of plunging his scythe through her heart. Azalea could still feel her chest frantically pounding as she leaned over to her phone to see what time it was. 3:52AM. If she didn't try to get back to sleep, she'd feel it in the morning. Resting her head back on the pillow, she lay there for a while contemplating. How different would life be if Poppy was still kicking? Would their mother still be her relaxed, stress-free self or would she still become the devil's advocate in a two-piece suit?

She knew, without a doubt, life would be completely different if Poppy had lived. Whilst part of her emotions tugged at her heart strings, wanting to wish her sister was still there, she was starting to doubt she wanted to change her life to how it could have been. As much as she missed her sister, she had finally started to open up about how she felt. She wasn't hiding her emotions from the world anymore, and that was all thanks to Tabby. Tabby had yanked open her shell and poked around inside until she found the pearl underneath. Tabby had willingly exposed her true self without a fear in the world, ready for the worst reaction possible. Tabby had kissed her back.

Thinking once more of Tabby's lips on her own, she raised her right hand to her face, her index finger gracefully stroking where Tabby had touched. She had acted like an idiot by kissing Tabby, but part of her longed to do it all over again. To tell Tabby she was falling for her. To tell Tabby that even without her make-up, her wig and the essential "pretty" kit she carried around in her backpack, she still saw her as the most beautiful girl in the world. To tell her she ached for every inch of her. As her brain teased the idea of more than a kissing embrace with Tabby, Azalea shook herself from her thoughts. She shouldn't think that way, especially with the girl she was thinking of a few feet away oblivious to her mind's obsession with removing her articles of clothing slowly, throwing them into a rough pile on the floor they could care about in the morning. She had to snap out of this loved-up, lustful trance. Staying there, right by Tabby's side, just brought out her dirtiest thoughts.

She was ashamed. Tabby was a friend, nothing more, nothing less, and she never wanted that to change. She was just projecting feelings onto her. That was all. She'd read that it could happen when people go through traumatic experiences. She didn't know how she felt inside; she just knew that right here right now in this moment she needed Tabby and her love. Pushing herself up off the half-sinking air mattress, she perched on the edge for a moment before placing her tippy toes on the fluffy carpet beneath her feet. Sneaking as noiselessly as she could, she left the room and headed across the corridor. Lightly pressing her palm to the centre of the door, it swung open effortlessly. The dusty smell with a hint of perfume welcomed her as she felt a slither of a breeze up her spine. Counting three lunges from the doorframe towards the centre of the vacant room, Azalea waited for the creak below her weight. As soon as she reached it, she lowered herself into a crouch and scratched her nails across the floorboards, searching until she felt a slight dip. Her mother would kill her if she knew that Azalea had kept some of Poppy's secrets even after death. Lightly lifting the board with one hand, the other swooped into the miniscule hole it formed. Tucked in a place that would never be found by a person who didn't know it existed. There was little that Poppy kept from the world, she was so open, but even she knew their mother wouldn't accept this. Unfolding the crumbled sheet of photo paper, a tear snuck down Azalea's cheek. Curling into the foetal position on the floor, she brought the picture to rest on her heart as she wept for a while. Lay with tears streaming down her face, she remained in that spot, the darkness finally overwhelming her.

She awoke as a beam of sunlight hit her face, blinding her good eye. The photo she had clung to throughout the night remained tucked between her fingertips. She knew she should hide it away once more in the secret spot but there was part of her that wanted to hold onto it a bit longer. Keeping it in her hand, she headed back to her own room, hoping everyone was still asleep.

Pushing her bedroom door ajar, she could see Tabby hadn't moved a muscle since she left hours earlier. Still lightly snoring away, duvet covering most of her face, Azalea could feel herself smiling. Not wanting to disturb her house guest, she crept over to her chest of drawers and opened her sock drawer. She placed the photo right at the back of the drawer. Thankfully, her mother had finally stopped snooping through her room so it was unlikely to be discovered unless she was dumb about it. With the secret all hidden away, she turned back to her mostly-deflated bed and grabbed her phone to wait for Tabby to roll out of bed.

Around 1PM, Tabby finally sheepishly joined the world of the living, all prepared for a day full of adventure. By half past, they'd already set off out for their last full day together. Azalea had planned in advance what they could do, knowing full well that Tabby's photography equipment would not be far behind. She seemed so fascinated with the area when they'd discussed the visit, she couldn't help but make a day just for the photographer's delight. Azalea dragged Tabby from location to location, finding pretty things she could capture in a flash. Buildings. Wildlife. Landscapes. The hours sped away and by the time the sun had started to sink behind the hills, the camera had eaten the life out of two sets of batteries.

As they walked home, arms interlinked, Tabby couldn't help but grin for the entire world to see. "You didn't have to make my final day all about me, you know?" she nudged her elbow into Azalea's side lightly; "We could have done anything in the universe."

"Unfortunately my spaceship's in the shop," Azalea smirked, "so space travel was off limits."

"You know what I mean, idiot." Tabby retorted, "You didn't have to do any of this. We could have just hung out in your room with movies and junk."

"And ruin what may be the last day of summer? We've not had rain in a week and we both know that never lasts in England. I'm expecting snow by morning." A chuckle turned into a chortle as the pair continued on their merry way back to the house.

"Thank you either way, Az", Tabby smiled, "For everything. You didn't have to do any of it. I'm glad to have a friend like you." Though the word friend shrunk her heart a little inside her chest, Azalea still let a smile glow on the outside. She didn't know what her own feelings were, but she wasn't going to let anything come between them. Not if she could help it.

Leaving you

Fills me with ache

With pain

With longing

Withdrawal wearing me thin

My mind a scratched record

Skipping to thoughts of you

I feel myself shutting down

My imagination flickers

My heart hibernates

My breath halts

Until I'm by your side

Your hand in mine

I'm alive again

Chapter 10

The morning Tabby left, Azalea was hesitant for the day to go on. Her alarm repeatedly echoed, blaring for the household to hear, until she finally gave in letting the morning start. She was so reluctant to walk by Tabby's side as she gabbled about what an exciting time Azalea would have when she visited her in a few weeks' time. She didn't want her to go. They still had so much to talk about. The visit had flown by too fast. Just another day, she pleaded with all the gods her mind could muster but no one acknowledged her plea. They waited and waited, trying to make the most out of their last few moments together, trying to conjure plans for when Azalea hit the city streets. She was so grateful her mother had agreed to let her visit when Tabby had suggested it at breakfast that morning. "A trip away with a friend sounds like a good idea, as long as you know it comes with rules," her mother sternly warned as they left out of the front door for the station. At quarter past 12, the train finally arrived at the platform. Tabby flung her arms tightly around Azalea and squeezed.

"I will see you as soon as you step off your train, I promise," she grinned at Azalea before lightly pecking her cheek. Stepping onto the train, Tabby settled in her carriage whilst Azalea watched on, hating every second of it. Leaving her side was the hardest part of the week for Azalea. As the train pulled out the station, she could feel the weight of her loneliness drooping over her once more. Retracing her steps to the entrance of the station, she hummed shyly to herself, ignoring the world around her. The floor was the only friend she needed at that moment, carrying her to where she needed to be.

Returning home, her room felt cool and desolate without Tabby's belongings flung all over the place. Even the cats couldn't be found in their usual hiding spots. It felt as if part of her had been ripped away once more, a feeling that became familiar after Poppy's death. Pacing over to the sock drawer, she took the photograph out. Part of her longed to tell their mother her eldest daughter's last secret, to unload the heavy bundle she held close to her heart, but she didn't know exactly what to say. *'Mum, I'm sorry but Poppy kept an important thing away from you and she died keeping it a secret'* didn't really have a ring to it. No part of what she had to say would be easy for her mother.

She cursed herself and her cowardice. She had clung to this last present Poppy had given her, but their mother had every right to know. She couldn't mourn something she didn't know existed and even though it might hurt, it wasn't her burden to bear alone. Tucking the photograph safely against her breast in her bra, she headed to the front room. She found her mother with two balls of fluff coating her, eyes closed and breathing lightly. She must be tired, she never napped. Azalea couldn't bring herself to wake her mother up. Sleep wasn't something that felt natural anymore in their household, so stealing it would be unfair. She crept around the sofa, pulling the blanket from the back over her mother to keep her warm and tucked her in lightly. Her mother's eyelids briefly fluttered but remained shut, peacefully unaware of the world around her.

Her mother's nap meant she at least had time to think about how to break the news. Her head was spiralling with all the positives and the negatives of laying the truth bare on the table. She didn't want to break her mother's heart but she knew that when the trial came in a few months' time everything would be out in the open. Every piece of her sister's dirty laundry, with anyone picking and prodding at the memory. They were just waiting for a confirmed date to relive the nightmare. The idea of sitting in the witness bench, being verbally harassed for hours, loomed over her and made her brain ache. She hoped she could bear the pressure.

She perched at the edge of the recliner, contemplating how to bring up the bombshell. She watched as the cats twitched and rolled on her mother, trying to find the comfiest spot. As Dali stretched and dug his claws into her mother's leg, she could see a grimace form in her mother's forehead wrinkles. Azalea rose and swiftly picked up Dali, a hand sweeping under his stomach, and pulled him into her chest. He glared at her, disappointed to be pulled away from his warm spot. She placed him gently on the ground before repeating the process with Storm.

Shaking her mother's shoulder, she prepared the words in her head before they could escape her lips. She needed this out in the open before it ate at her any further. Especially before she lost her nerve. "Azalea?" her mother tiredly questioned, her eyes still hazed from her mid-afternoon nap. She blew a few loose strands of hair off of her face, trying to completely focus on her daughter.

"Mum," Azalea took a deep breath, her hand struggling to grasp the picture in her bra. "There's something I need to tell you." Her mother looked at her confused, though she wasn't sure if it was half-asleep fog still affecting her. Azalea unfolded the photograph and placed it on the centre of the coffee table for her mother to see. The tears were escaping her tear ducts before her mother had a proper chance to comprehend what was in front of her.

There on the table in black and white lay a crumpled sonogram, Poppy's full name printed on the top. Her mother edged closer, her face struck with grief eyes widening, as she made out the shape of the unborn grandchild she would never know.

◆━━━━━━━━━━━━━━━━━●━━━━━━━━━━━━━━━━━◆

At no point prior did Azalea consider just how her mother would react to the news when she eventually had to spill it. It had been two days since she'd laid the sonogram flat for the world to see but she had still not heard her mother utter a word since. At least not to her, though she did hear whisperings coming from her mother's room the night before. Seeing her mother's face contort with so much pain caused her own heart to break even further. She felt deeply that her mother needed to know and deserved to know just as much as she did, but the reveal had left her regretting her decision. She should have waited and prayed to every god that her mother would never need to know.

She knew the police were aware of her sister's state but she'd pled at her initial interview with the homicide team that they not tell her. The death of Poppy had already torn life from her mother, she wasn't prepared for the police to hand her a personalised noose just for her to swing from. They'd agreed much to their own annoyance to her desperate pleas not to admit the pregnancy to her mother but urged repeatedly for Azalea to discuss it with her mother prior to the court date. With Hunter pleading not guilty at his initial hearing, all the evidence was being placed on the table, baby and all.

The inaudible suspense was indulging itself on Azalea's sanity as she waited for her mother to speak. Her mother, the loud booming woman that she was, could not hold her tongue for eternity. That Azalea knew to be fact. She'd expected "how", "what", "where", "why", "when" and "who", not the silent treatment she'd received. The standard interrogation questioning she saved for Azalea's everyday life, not the mute air that hung in their home. As the seconds ticked by, she tensed more. She felt like a small child, waiting to be punished for foiled pranks. Yet no response ever came. Her mother got to her feet, leaving the sonogram on the table, and head to her bedroom to not return for the entirety of the day. Azalea waited for a few hours, hoping her mother would at least come back and sit with her again and discuss how she was feeling – the exact thing she had been urging Azalea to do – but she never came back. Her bedroom door remained shut, not even a hint of noise slipping under the door.

As they sat in pure silence on the third morning of the silent treatment, an arm length's distance between them at the dining room table, Azalea could hear her inner-self pleading with her mother. Her cereal lay soggy and untouched in the bowl in front of her, her spoon still on the table dry. She couldn't think of what to say, or what to do. Not with her mother like this. It was as if she were shell-shocked to the core.

"Please say something," she found herself bellowing in her mother's direction as she sat sipping her tea. Her mother placed her mug on the table and glared at her from across the dining room table. A dark fury was burning in her mother's eyes and she knew that her request was going to bite back with a moment's notice.

"What do you expect me to say?!" her mother hissed angrily. "That I'm pissed off? That I want that monster to be executed for what he did? That I can't believe that Poppy kept something so important from me? That I can't believe you wouldn't tell me sooner?" The questions fired rapidly, each bullet piercing Azalea's heart. Bullseye. "Why wasn't I told by the police? Surely *that* couldn't have been missed on an autopsy. Why didn't she tell me? I'm her mother. Why couldn't she?" The tears couldn't be held in any longer. They streamed down her mother's face, splashing against the table's surface as she rested her forehead in her hands. Reaching her hand across the table, Azalea sighed, her tongue too tied to speak.

"Why didn't she tell me, Az?" Her mother sobbed, her shoulders shaking as she sat back up in her chair. "Why didn't you?"

She could feel herself getting worked up as she looked at her mother. She willed her tear ducts to remain dry. She took a deep breath, allowing herself a moment to think of the best way to put it. "It wasn't my news to tell, mum," she shrugged uncontrollably. "Poppy didn't even tell me. I found the test." She hoped her mother hadn't learnt her poker face because the lie was kinder than the truth.

"If I tell you something, Azzie, will you promise not to tell anyone? Not even mum?" Poppy innocently whispered in her ear one afternoon, an excited little bop in her movement. Azalea hadn't seen Poppy that giddy in so long, she was eager to share her sister's secret, even if she had to take it to her grave. Her happiness was almost contagious.

"Pop, this better not be something stupid. I've got things to do, people to see. I'm a busy girl, you know," she pouted exaggeratedly to her sister. She couldn't hold in her laughter though, not where Poppy was involved, a smile soon forming on her face. "Go on, tell me," she urged, "I can't wait forever."

"You, Azalea Rose Hart, are going to be an auntie!"

Azalea's jaw hit the floor. She hadn't expected that, or for Poppy to be so happy about it. Poppy hadn't been home for long, having only just finally escaping the clutches of her abusive ex-boyfriend. She didn't want Poppy to spiral back into his world by being trapped by his DNA.

"Is it…?" She hesitated, not wanted to speak his name aloud even then. Something about him, aside from the obviously evil nature, had put Azalea off Hunter since day 1 even if she used to fancy him. What he'd done to Poppy was not acceptable. She needed better. He didn't deserve a first chance with her sister and she hoped this revelation didn't encourage a second one.

"Yes, but he doesn't know and if I can help it, he never will." A sigh of relief escaped Azalea's lips. "And anyway, he's not allowed near me, remember? Restraining order and all that." After the last incident, Azalea was glad there was a restraining order preventing him for approaching her sister. At the time, she'd thought maybe the hospital visit with a busted nose and a few broken ribs had been her sister's wake up call, but maybe it was something different.

"Why don't you want to tell mum?" Azalea curiously questioned. Poppy never kept anything from their mother. It almost made Azalea sick how close the two of them were. They were practically in sync.

"If she knew, she'd worry. You know how she is." Poppy shook her head lightly, hair shaking everywhere. "Please, Az, promise you won't say anything?" Poppy urged, desperation in her eyes as she passed the sonogram to Azalea. Since Poppy came back, their mother had kept her on a short leash as a just-in-case to keep her safe at home away from Hunter and his acquaintances. If their mother found out now, the extremely limited freedom Poppy had would disappear in a flash. Azalea couldn't do that to Poppy. She knew she needed freedom after being practically imprisoned.

"Fine," Azalea shrugged, "But she'll murder you when she finds out, especially when she finds out I knew before her," she joked as her sister smacked her arm playfully. Poppy smiled warmly at her, before pulling her into a tight embrace.

Thinking back, Azalea regretted her words. She should never have joked something like that would happen to Poppy. She felt like she jinxed her almost.

I'm forgetting

How it feels to have you close

To my side always attached to my hip

Your words delicately spoken

To me and me alone

The world did not need to hear your secrets

The truth only we knew

I feel as if the real me is fading

Replaced with a being that barely exists without you

Every day I feel paler, softer, lighter

Closer to the point

Where I do not exist

But am the faint memory

For the cycle to start again

For someone else to bear

Chapter 11

After the breakdown the other day, things at home appeared to be as normal as ever. Azalea kept to herself, her mother checking in with her regularly to ensure she was fine. Sleep. Eat. Life. Repeat. That remained their pattern for the next few weeks as Azalea prepared, almost counting down the days, until she next saw Tabby. She packed, unpacked and repacked her bags what felt like a billion times. She'd never really slept anywhere aside from family homes and holiday caravans until the counselling trip. No sleepovers, no school trips – no way to know what to possibly expect.

Of course, she'd seen Poppy attend such things – Poppy was popular in school and fit in with everyone so naturally she was invited to participate in everything – but there was a big difference between a sleepover with two other thirteen year old girls with junk food and rom coms to staying with a girl who left her confused all over alone with no parental supervision. Still on the 23rd of July, she found herself travelling to the train station, slowly placing one foot in front of the other, as if even the smallest crack in the ground will pull her under, engulfing her, preventing her from existing outside of her small town's bubble.

Hovering around the platform, she watched the station's clock tick by. 34 minutes and 18 seconds until the train would whisk her away to the big, old city. 34 minutes and 15 seconds until she could tell Tabby she was on her way. 34 minutes and 9 seconds until she started to panic about the journey. 34 minutes and 4 seconds until she felt the rush of blood in her ears telling her it was a bad idea to do this, to turn back, go back home and curl up in bed forever. 33 minutes and 53 seconds until the nausea joined in, reminding her she was well and truly going to be out of her comfort zone. Busy public, rumbling traffic and constant distractions weren't something she enjoyed and she was heading straight towards it. 33 minutes and 26 seconds to convince herself to give up now.

She knew if she let her panic take over, she would never even place her pinky toe on the floor of the train carriage never mind her entire self. She had to control herself. She decided to focus elsewhere. On other passengers waiting. On the shadows dancing to the silent ballet on the platform's dingy stone, interlacing intricately with the most gruesome of the stains it was coated in. Her eyes finally caught the sight of a toddler, no more than two with bobbing blonde curls, unsteadily waddling towards her father, who held his arms open wide a small distance away. The little girl, giggling profusely darted into his embrace without a moment of hesitation. Azalea wished she could be that decisive. She was insanely jealous. Maybe her life could have been different if she had a positive male role model. Maybe Poppy wouldn't have ended up how she did, cremated at the age of 21. Maybe Azalea wouldn't have felt completely isolated. Maybe she would have known how to deal with her grief in an effective manner instead of shutting out the world. Maybe her confidence would have been more than zilch.

No, she shook the thought from her mind; her mother did a fine job raising two young girls all on her own. She didn't need a father to be whole or to fix all her problems with the power of existence. Having a more involved paternal figure would not have changed her in any way. She would have still ended up this broken in the end, possibly even more so. If she asked for her mother's opinion, it would be simply worded as "fuck men" or "you don't need men to be happy." Her mother seemed to have survived without her father by her side so she could live on just the same. She glanced at the clock once more. 6 minutes until the train arrived. At least the thought of the man who abandoned her distracted her for a short while.

The train ride wasn't as bad as she had thought it would be. Though it became cramped within a matter of minutes Azalea kept herself in her safe little bubble, the idea of Tabby keeping her going. She didn't want to let her down by coming so far but failing before the final hurdle. She dug her nails into her hands; bit her lip; played with her hair under her fingertips - doing all she could to distract herself from the carriage constantly bumping roughly on the tracks as she headed further South than she was used to. She managed, thankfully, to grab a seat at least. She wasn't sure she could last more than a minute with the sardines that were crushed against one another in the standing portion.

The thick groups slowly dispersed, stop by stop, as the train plodded along on its' path. Azalea closely watched the stops, anxious hers will come and go in a matter of moments before she had the chance to exit. The few people who remained around her appeared oblivious to their current location, almost as if they were running on automatic pilot. Knowing her stop was close, she collected her belongings and headed towards the door. Someone quickly pounced in the warm seat she'd left behind. Greedy people were always so quick in someone else's grave to get what they want, she thought to herself. Not long after, the train halted at her stop and she exited swiftly not wanting to be crushed as people rushed in all directions.

Standing on the station's platform, she frantically searched for her companion. Tabitha, she cursed in her head, you promised. Glancing at her phone, she hoped there'd be a text but there was nothing new, just the usual app updates. She rose to her tippy toes, eager for a height advantage over the clusters of human mass. There, in the distance, she saw a rush of blonde heading in her direction. A squeal burst from her lips as she heard her name bellowed from the blur running at her.

"Tabby!" she grinned, ear to ear, as tell practically collapsed at her feet.

"My love, my darling, my all – I apologise deeply for standing you up for a mere second. The taxi was an absolute nightmare to add onto the mess that is already my life." Tabby panted, trying to breathe between words. Azalea blushed; Tabby could be so dramatic at times.

Still flustered in the face, Tabby pulled Azalea in close and squeezed her tight. "I've missed you, pet, it feels like a lifetime."

Her blush hitting a shade of deep crimson, Azalea smiled at Tabby as she pulled away. "Likewise, Tabbs. So, now that you are finally here – what is the plan?"

"Firstly," Tabby smirked, linking her arm with Azalea's and grabbing the bags without hesitation, "I'm going to take you back to my home where we will indulge in the sweetest of all cakes – milk and white chocolate marble cake with a thick ganache." Tabby licked her lower lip hungrily. "Then, the world is ours to conquer!"

Stood outside, Tabby's block of flats looked intimidating. Azalea tried counting the floors, but gave up shortly after 18. It seemed to go on forever into the sky and she hoped she wouldn't be staying at the top of a tower block for a week – whilst she was not afraid of heights per se, she wouldn't want a bad turn with such a drop.

Tabby beckoned silently for Azalea to follow her inside with a slight nod of her head. As she followed, she took in her surroundings. The peeling paint in the hallways. The out of order sign covered in dust hanging on the immobile lift doors. Azalea begrudgingly dragged her baggage up the 13 flights of stairs regretting every item which weighed it down until they finally reached it. Tabby's flat. As the door to flat 13B was unlocked, Azalea half-expected the flat to be as seamlessly decrepit as the rest of the building but the first thing that drew her in was the mural that was sketched on the wall in the main hallway. A mix of pastels as a backdrop helped the elegant phoenix - glittering with fierce bronzes, silvers and golds amongst crimson feathers - that flew above her stand out in comparison to the rest of the bland walls. "My spirit animal," she recalled Tabby saying once as they spoke late into the early hours. Of course it had to be a central part of her humble abode.

The front room itself was less spectacular – full of dark hues, cluttered with undisguisable furnishings that looked as if you could pick it up from any housing store. The flat pack furniture and overworked microwave added to the essential student experience. Azalea placed her belongings by the tiny coffee table as Tabby led her around the rest of the facilities, meaning the only other two rooms in the flat.

They settled in for the afternoon, a large cake and a pot of tea between them as they enjoyed whatever daytime TV played in the background as they got up-to-date with each other's lives. Azalea smiled. It partially felt like coming home to an old friend, even if there was a slight difference in the air.

The days blurred as Azalea followed Tabby around the unfamiliar setting like a puppy nervously trailing its' owner afraid of a misstep. They explored museums, parks, the city centre. Perfect places for Azalea to practice her scenic photography. Part of her couldn't settle though. As much as she'd missed Tabby and wanted to enjoy their time together, especially if it involved a great piece of architecture and her beloved camera, the city frightened her in ways she'd never imagined. The loud noises, the bright lights, the bustling crowds. She missed her little town. She felt exhausted. The constant busyness of the world around her kept thoughts and sounds creeping into her unguarded subconscious. She couldn't focus when she tried to shoot, no matter how hard she tried. There was always little distractions putting her off, destroying the precious seconds.

Since she'd arrived, she could have sworn she'd heard Poppy's shrieks more than once when they'd been walking through the general masses. Every sharp breeze and exhaust failure made her jump. She felt herself counting every time people got too close, which appeared inevitable in the daily hustle and bustle of the city streets. Her mind was in hyperdrive and it showed no sign of slowing down.

When she looked at Tabby though, it appeared she took no notice. Part of Tabby seemed as distracted as she was. She wondered what could possibly be running through her friend's mind and if it was as haunting as her own. As Azalea watched Tabby's actions closely, every breath every step, there was no obvious signs as to what was bothering her friend. Not until the third day.

The morning started just like the previous days. Azalea was woken after a groggy night of tossing and turning, counting the ceiling tiles and praying to a mythical being for some dreamless rest. She wasn't sure which was worse, her surroundings or what they caused her brain to conjure when she finally had those 3 seconds of untroubled sleep of just blank darkness behind her eyelids. She glanced at the now-empty spot beside her. When she'd finally drifted, Tabby was by her side, cradling a beaten teddy bear missing a paw. Now her partner in crime was nowhere to be seen.

Pushing her toes into Tabby's spare slippers, she forced herself to her feet and began to explore. Listening for any sign of life, Azalea could hear quiet whisperings coming from the front door. Glancing around the corner, she could see Tabby frantically whispering down the phone, tears in her eyes, as she focused delicately on the words coming from the other end of the phone. She didn't know what to do. Part of her wanting to rush to Tabby's side, sit next to her and hear what was wrong but the rest of her knew it was wrong to eavesdrop on an obviously private conversation. She crept back to the bedroom and got changed, pretending she had never left in the first place.

Chapter 12

Tabby didn't seem herself after the phone call. She was unworldly silent as she sat across from Azalea in the front room, pillow on her lap, pulling loose threads with her nails tweezed. Azalea was fighting the urge to ask. She knew if it was important, if Tabby wanted her to know, she'd be told in an instant. She did not need to pry but Tabby's current reaction was scaring her. She has never seen her so quiet, so zoned out of reality.

Hesitantly, Azalea glanced up at the girl she thought of as her best friend. "Tell me," she projected in Tabby's direction, unable to make proper contact. The words flew over Tabby's head as she remained in oblivion. "Tabitha, tell me," she urged louder, more focused.

Tabby looked at Azalea, a deadness resting in her pupils. "There's nothing to tell," she murmured, her hands fidgeting in front of her.

"Bullshit!" Azalea squealed, "Tabby, you are not being yourself. Please let me help you! I'm here for you, you know I am!" She perched on the end of her seat, in case she needed to jump up and comfort Tabby at any moment.

"Fuck off, Azalea." Tabby snarled. "You don't know me, you don't know if I'm being myself or not." Tabby glared at her, a look of hatred shining through her normally sweet façade.

Azalea remained seated, not sure how to react. She looked at her own hands, starting to shake, starting to twitch. "Tabby, I know you," she whispered anxiously, "And I want to help."

"There's nothing you can fucking do, Az. There's no point in you being here. You can't help me. Doctors can't help me. The fucking pope couldn't help me, no matter how hard he tried. I am beyond help." Tabby rose to her feet. She paced across the room, not glancing in Azalea's direction as she moved. She picked up a ceramic mug and angrily threw it at the empty wall across from her. As it shattered, both girls winced at the sound.

"Just leave, Az. Just fuck right off. Go. Get the fuck out. I don't need you. I don't need anyone. Just go." Tabby repeated the words, as if on a loop as she went around, distressing the already somewhat distressed room more. Ripping the paper off the walls, throwing breakables against the floors and walls, punching everything and anything that would break. Her anger just increased the more her face flushed.

With every smash Azalea fled the direction, not wanting to be hit. "Tabby, you're making no sense. What the fuck is wrong with you?" Her words came out more poisonous than she aimed with too much toxicity in her voice. Tabby looked in her direction and seemed to look through her entirely. As if she no longer existed in Tabby's eyes.

"A lot is fucking wrong with me!" Tabby roared, "But it doesn't fucking matter to you. Get the fuck out of my flat, right fucking now!"

"Tabby, please," Azalea pleaded. "Help me understand what is up. I want to help. Don't leave it like this!"

"I don't want you in my life, Az. I'm worthless, you're worthless. This 'friendship'," quotation marks gestured with her slinky fingers, "is absolutely pointless. You don't get me and I don't want you to even fucking try. Leave. I won't tell you again."

"Please, Tabby," Azalea pleaded more, tears starting to form in the corner of her eyes, "I'm sorry, I didn't mean to pry."

"Just grab your shit and go, Az." Tabby hissed, "I don't want to see you again." Tabby left the room to come back a moment later, shoes on, coat over her shoulder. She looked once more at Azalea and headed out the door, leaving Azalea in the devastation of her wake.

As her taxi pulled into the train station, Azalea tried to figure out just what she did wrong. She thought long and hard and other than pushing a potentially awkward conversation, she couldn't see what had gone wrong between her and Tabby. If only Tabby had spoken to her. If only she'd not pushed it too far. She checked her phone incessantly. Still no messages from Tabby, though she didn't know what she expected. She didn't know what had caused Tabby to flip out, so why would she text after such an episode? She sighed heavily. The first proper friend she'd had and she may have lost her due to her own stupidity of pressuring things out of people. Habits she used to have with Poppy died hard.

She called her mother, just to let her know to expect her home. Her mother questioned her, asking what was wrong. Why was she home early? Did she need to be met? Was she safe? Was Tabby okay? Azalea felt herself on the verge of cracking as she spoke to her mother. She simply replied she'd speak to her when she got home as it was a complicated situation. She hoped to have her own answers by the time she'd finally reached her house.

By the time she pushed her front door open, the cats darting at her feet, she still hadn't heard anything from Tabby. She sniffled, fighting back the urge to cry. I hope she's okay, Azalea thought to herself, even though she knew it didn't matter. Tabby had made it clear she didn't want Azalea in her life anymore. Plopping her belongings at the foot of the stairs, Azalea headed to the seatee and curled into a ball hoping it was all just a bad dream and that she'd still be with Tabby, no elephant in the room between them. As she remained curled, she dosed off and the cats came and claimed her as their comfy pillow for the evening.

Chapter 13

She wanted to throw her phone against the wall. Her chest hurt from how hard her heart was racing. The calls felt almost back to back, even if they were hours apart. When it first buzzed early that morning, she knew something was wrong. There had to be something wrong. No one calls at half 5 in the morning with good news.

"Tab, it's your grandpa," she could hear Bernie, the assistant manager at his care home Crimson Meadows sigh heavily and sleepily, "He's had another accident."

"What type of accident?" She whispered, crawling out of bed hoping she didn't wake Az up with all her movement. The vibrating on the bedside table hadn't thankfully. The girl appeared to sleep like she was a corpse.

"He was having a bad day yesterday and well, it seemed he didn't shake it."

Her grandfather wasn't in great shape to begin with, mentally or physically. Alzheimer's had truly taken him down and left him as a hollow existence. Only on the greatest days did he remember her mother's name enough to think Tabby was her, never mind on the bad ones when everything around became dangerous in his hands. She'd lost count how many times he'd hit her with a belt across the face whilst she fought him into clothes before she and her social worker finally decided a care home with the right care and medication was the best option for him, even if she ended up in care for the next 5 years. Nurses and carers at his beck and call with no angsty teenage granddaughters to make his life difficult. Of course, neither she nor her grandfather expected him to be her only living relative as she hit puberty, but neither party could help it.

"Where is he, Bern?" She longed for the simplest of answers. She knew it was incredibly unlikely, but she wished her grandfather was tucked in his bed being regularly monitored but sleeping through his bad moments.

"We've had to send him to hospital, Tab - he's split his head open. He's at Saint Edward's on Cross Street, ward 50. They're keeping him in for observation. Tab…" Tabby could hear the hesitation in Bernie's voice. The bad news was coming, she could feel it in her bones.

"Spit it out already," she heard herself hiss with venom into the receiver. It was too early for all of this shit. The waiting made it ten times worse.

"We can't care for him anymore, chuck," Bernie murmured on the other end of the phone, "He's nearly put another one of our nurses in the hospital with an outburst. You know how it is. He's gotten worse and his care really needs to be stepped up."

"Please don't say what I think you're going to say, Bern. Please don't do that to me." Tabby could hear her voice shaking as she knew what was coming next. If her grandfather's care home couldn't look after him any more as his condition had gotten too severe, that meant he was being shipped away, past her grasp.

"He has to go there, Tabby. You know we can't put it off any longer. With you being his next of kin..." Tabby could clearly hear the reluctance in Bernie's voice as she fought herself to allow the next words to come forward "You need to sign the consent forms for his transfer."

She couldn't help the tears as they flooded silently down her cheeks. Her last family member was being taken away. The only person she'd had since she was 6. Since the world cruelly took away both of her parents on the same night at the hands of a drunk driver and a patch of black ice on that mid-December evening.

"Please, Bern, don't send him away. Not yet." Her words came out as whimpers and she was unsure if the other woman could hear her over how hard she was frantically panting trying to keep the waterfalls billowing from her eyes in.

"Tabby, I can't. Saint Augustine's facility is the best place for him. We told you if his condition worsened, he couldn't stay forever. Especially after last time."

The last time her grandfather had a bad day, he'd broken the nose and split the lip of a nursing student who just happened to be in the wrong place at the wrong time. He was in the middle of a delusion and thought she was death, coming to take him for good. She'd begged and pleaded for her grandfather to stay at the home that time, but she knew one more episode would do it. This was the episode that pushed it too far and Saint Augustine's was his last option. Crimson Meadows were the only people willing to open their doors to him to begin with so she had no other local option, and having a specialised team looking after her grandfather would at least leave Tabby feeling more comforted. The only reason she couldn't stand the idea of her grandfather moving to Saint Augustine's was the distance. From what she remembered from the brochure her social worker showed her when they were first discussing the best place for him, it was around a few hundred miles away with no access from public transport anywhere in sight. Tabby couldn't afford to pick up her life and follow her grandfather's shadow to wherever it may lay. She was stuck where she was and there was nothing she could do about it.

The only reason she even had a roof over her head currently, as shabby as it was, was because her mother had smartly made her grandfather do a will when he first became what her mother referred to in a homemade video she found as "a little ditsy in the memory region". Whilst the rest of his will covered his medical expenses and his care home choice, the flat was entirely hers – it was a shame it was practically worthless.

Tabby swallowed the lump that lurked in her throat and took a deep breath. She knew sooner or later she had to say the words Bernie was waiting to hear.

"Okay, Bernie. Get the paperwork sorted. I'll visit my grandad then I'll be over and we'll get it in motion." Bernie made some other noises but Tabby's brain couldn't focus on it. The call dropped shortly after as Tabby remained huddled in the hallway.

She was still sat on the floor when the phone started ringing again. Thinking it was Bernie calling back with an update, she answered it without even glancing at the screen. "Hello?"

"Hi, is this Tabitha Dixon?" the voice on the other end of the line questioned.

"Yes?" she responded hesitantly. No one who had her number ever used her full name, not since she'd finished high school.

"It's Lucy from the firm of Henderson and Oates." Tabby felt every muscle in her body tense up. She hadn't heard from the solicitors in a long, long time. She could feel the storm brewing as she had to put extra effort into breathing.

"What can I do for you, Lucy?" Her response was almost autonomous. She didn't want to press the conversation further and longed to hang up but her voice and shaking hands wouldn't let her.

"I can imagine you're shocked to hear from us. I know it's been some time, just over 2 years I believe. But we promised we'd keep you updated, which is why I'm calling. I apologise for the early hour. Did I wake you?" She could hear the faked concern in Lucy's voice. It didn't matter whether she'd been woken or not, Lucy was just doing her job pushing buttons at the other end of a phone line, frustrating people as early as 7.30 in the morning it seemed.

"Well I'm guessing it doesn't matter if it's urgent enough to call me now," Tabby found herself rolling her eyes, even though Lucy couldn't see her. She pulled her knees into her chest, one arm wrapped around them tightly, waiting to hear the worst.

"He's getting released on good behaviour, Tabitha. He appealed his sentence, got it reduced to 4 years and since he's served half already..." Tabby didn't want to hear the rest. Her head blocked out the voice on the phone and focused heavily on her racing heartbeat. He couldn't be released. Not yet. She was supposed to have planned her escape from this stupid city. Distanced herself completely from the past. Sold this flat and moved further afield. Not too far so she could still visit her grandad, but not close enough to run into Olly in the corner shop buying cornflakes.

She found herself once more sitting at the long table at the firm's office. Lucy touch-typing the meeting as they both listened to

Jayda, the hotshot solicitor who promised Tabby a safe life ahead, as she explained the court case to them. Tabby scratched automatically at her itchy scalp and wished she hadn't. The scars were too new, too sensitive. The slightest touch made it feel like she was being burnt all over again.

.

"I've spoken with the prosecutor, who in turn has spoken to the judge. It's been agreed with the defence that if Oliver pleads guilty to the domestic abuse and the grievous bodily harm, he'll serve 9 years." Jayda looked Tabby in the eye, confidence flaming behind her hazel eyes.

"I know you wanted more, and you deserve a lot more than what is on the table, but I know you don't want to take that witness stand and if we push for more you'll be up there at a moment's notice. We can do everything we can so you don't have to see him but we can't promise the defence won't grill every single choice you've ever made in your life, and we both know Tabitha you have made quite a few very questionable, very illegal life choices." Jayda stood and walked around the table, pacing from the wall to the door, waiting for any form of response from Tabby.

Tabby couldn't take her eyes off the table. All she wanted to do was scratch her skin away. She wasn't sure if it was the withdrawals hitting hard or being told that the man who used her as a punching bag for as long as they were together could be walking free before she'd even turned 30. Her reflection in the shiny glossed surface looked just as haunted as she felt. She glanced briefly at Lucy, sat at the other side of the table watching her intently, waiting to note down her next words as precisely as possible. Looking Lucy in the eyes for that moment, she wasn't sure if what she saw back was sympathy, pity or curiosity.

"I'll take whatever I can get." Tabby pulled herself to her feet, flung her bag on her shoulder and started to leave the room before it closed in on her. "Just let me know how it goes." She called behind her, slamming the door in tow. Neither Jayda or Lucy followed her as she left the building and merged with the busy foot traffic on the pavement. She walked as fast as she could and swiftly exited into an alley as soon as she felt she was far enough away.

She crumbled behind an industrial-sized dustbin and started to rummage through her bag. She pulled out a bottle of vodka, undid the lid and glugged a fifth of the bottle away in a minute. She continued to rummage until she found enough pills to keep her going until she made it home. Throwing them back, the vodka helping them down, she stood once more and started to head home. She knew she had to stop the drinking and all the pills, but there was no way she could do that until he was behind bars. She needed the brief release they gave her.

Every part of Tabby was urging her to find the closest source of relief. She regretted her lack of alcohol in the flat. She longed for a bottle of Jack Daniels or a can of some fruity cider to keep her going. She found herself wondering if she'd really disposed of everything on her clean crusade. She searched every little crack, trying her hardest to be as silent as a mouse as to not wake Azalea. She felt like a starving animal, looking for a crumb to sustain her. Finally, after pulling up some loose floorboards, she found a small, slightly dusty bag of white powder. Without hesitation, the substance was gone. She went and sat down in the front room, waiting for her blood stream to pump around the relief to every cell of her body.

A few minutes, or possibly even hours later she wasn't sure, Azalea sat across from her. Tabby pulled at the pillow that had found its way onto her lap, grasping at the loose strands between her nails and pulling them out, thread by thread. She almost didn't hear Azalea at first, too focused on the thread and the sound of her blood rushing through her veins.

"Tabitha, tell me," she could hear the desperation in Azalea's voice and found herself making eye contact. She didn't want

Azalea to realise that she'd lost control, that she'd given in to the urge to fill herself with toxic chemicals again.

"There's nothing to tell," she found herself murmuring. How exactly could she explain it anyway? 'Sorry, Az, someone has just dropped an atom bomb on my existence' didn't seem to cover just how much devastation those calls had caused. Her head wouldn't shut off, no matter how hard she tried. The more she tried to push it away, the more she remembered. Every bruise, every blood curdling scream, every lame excuse. She moved her hands from the pillow and starting picking at her own fingers, hoping the pinching and pulling might make her feel better. Sometimes some self-induced pain was good like that.

"Bullshit!" the squeal squeakily escaped Azalea's lips, "Tabby, you are not being yourself. Please let me help you! I'm here for you, you know I am!" Watching her, Tabby could see Azalea gripping to the edge of her seat. She knew that the girl meant well, but she was being no help. Tabby had tried for years to prepare for this and nothing had helped. She knew the words of a teenager who had a slightly common tragic backstory wouldn't be enough to keep her going. At that point, Tabby knew that she was no good for this girl who was in the process of recovering herself. She was on a downward spiral with every memory of Olly and his terror flooding back and she didn't wish to take an innocent girl down with her.

"Fuck off, Azalea." She snarled, trying to force a toughness she had to dig deep for. "You don't know me, you don't know if I'm being myself or not." She glared at Azalea, trying hard to ignore Olly's words of hatred as her brain whispered them at her.

. "Tabby, I know you," Azalea whispered anxiously, "And I want to help."

Azalea's words tugged at Tabby's heartstrings. She truly loved this girl, but she couldn't cope. She didn't deserve friends, as Olly told her often. He was the only person she needed and she was nothing without him. Just a worthless speck of shit on the planet.

"There's nothing you can fucking do, Az. There's no point in you being here. You can't help me. Doctors can't help me. The fucking pope couldn't help me, no matter how hard he tried. I am beyond help." Tabby rose to her feet starting to pace. She fought the urge to look Azalea's way, to run to the comfort she was being offered. She needed to scare her enough so that she'd run and never come back. It wasn't safe for Azalea to be part of Tabby's world anymore. Not if he was free. Not if his words and actions were no longer submerged to the depths of her memories. She grabbed the closest thing to her, a ceramic mug, and threw it against the wall opposite her. In that moment, all she wanted to do was tear down everything around her until it was all as broken as she felt.

"Just leave, Az. Just fuck right off. Go. Get the fuck out. I don't need you. I don't need anyone. Just go." Tabby continued, repeating the words hoping they'd hit home. She continued to destroy everything in her path as she walked around her living quarters as she fought the ongoing battle in her. The flashes that were haunting her now made her want to run but she knew Azalea had to be gone first. She has to be safe away from her.

Azalea ran around the room, avoiding the objects Tabby was throwing wildly around the room. "Tabby, you're making no sense. What the fuck is wrong with you?" There was so much poison in those words that Tabby knew she'd finally hit the mark. She could finally save Azalea from herself. Another flash hit her. A millisecond of her pinned to this very spot.

"A lot is fucking wrong with me!" Tabby roared at Azalea, pushing as far as she could. Another flash, she could feel the bruises along her jawline as the shadow glared over her. "But it doesn't fucking matter to you. Get the fuck out of my flat, right fucking now!"

"Tabby, please," The other girl pleaded, every syllable sounded as if she was holding back tears. "Help me understand what is up. I want to help. Don't leave it like this!"

"I don't want you in my life, Az. I'm worthless, you're worthless. This 'friendship'," she quoted in the air, "is absolutely pointless. You don't get me and I don't want you to even fucking try. Leave. I won't tell you again." Another flash, and she could feel her clothes forcefully removed as she heard her own voice plead for it to stop, for him to just leave her be for one night.

"Please, Tabby," Azalea pleaded more and as Tabby watched on the tears started to form in the corner of Azalea's eyes to the point they were a second away from flooding, "I'm sorry, I didn't mean to pry."

"Just grab your shit and go, Az, I don't want to see you again." Tabby knew she had to leave. She couldn't watch Azalea leave when her heart was still telling her to turn around and apologise. It pled for her to explain everything but Tabby knew as soon as she did, there was no way Azalea would ever leave her side. She returned to the room once more, shoes on and ready to leave. She looked once more at Azalea and then left as fast as her feet would take her. Another flash came, just as she reached her door, of his fist slamming into her face and the darkness that followed. She needed out of that flat before every single memory of Olly made her want to torch down the only place she ever felt she could truly call home. She should never have let that monster into her home, or her bed. She fidgeted with her coat, making sure she had her ID in her jacket pocket, and headed for the corner shop. She had over a year's worth of sobriety she was ready to flush down the toilet with the cheapest bottle of booze she could find.

Chapter 14

Azalea felt completely restless. It had been a month since she'd last seen Tabby and she hadn't heard anything since. She wasn't sure if she was dead or alive at this point thanks to Tabby abstaining from social media. She was too nervous to text her, fearing the rejection of a 'read' message flashing with no response. She constantly regretted prying into a part of Tabby's life it was clear she didn't belong. She missed her friend dearly and wished she'd taken the other path. She needed a friend at a time like this.

Her own life was becoming a disaster. With the court case nearing closer by the day, Poppy's murder lingered in the air everywhere she went. She knew sooner or later she'd be stood in court, recounting every second she couldn't do anything for her sister. The prosecutor wasn't making anything easier. Every other day, she sat at her kitchen table being interrogated by a grumpy-looking man in a bland beige suit.

Whilst she had no particular opinion of Arthur Strickland, the main prosecutor, his assistant was a different matter altogether. A balding man with ginger stubble which resembled that of a teenage boy's, Paul Archer was slowly becoming Azalea's depiction of the devil himself. Whilst his boss was around, he behaved like an obedient servant but as soon as he and Felicity were out of the way, his personality changed. The mild-mannered attitude he presented with became ultimately sadistic. She knew that without Paul's help she may completely mess up her witness statement during the cross examination, but she couldn't believe that anyone else in the world would ever force so much pain on another human being. Every time tears appeared in the corner of her eyes, Paul smirked. He was enjoying every moment of making her relive the worst event in her life.

On the fifteenth visit Paul and Arthur made to the Hart household, Azalea was prepared. She'd forced herself to relive the experience so many times now, there was no way it could hurt her further. The usual bombardment of questions started the practice as they sat across from each other. Paul demanded on the first visit that she make eye contact during the entirety. He said it was prepare her for the court room but Azalea knew he was just adding the pain from her eyes to his memory for future use.

"On the night in question, why was Poppy home alone?" This was one of his favourite questions, she'd noticed. He wanted to focus on how Poppy was, as he'd previously worded it, 'abandoned' by her family on the last night of her life.

Azalea fought hard to focus on Paul's eyes. She knew if she even glanced away at the start, she'd lose. "It was Halloween evening, my mother was at a party at her friend's and I'd gone to find our cat. Poppy wasn't supposed to be home, or alone, she was on her way to a party."

"And her behaviour," he pushed, "was it in any way suspicious? Did it seem like she had other plans, that she was sneaking around that night with someone she said she wouldn't?" Since the first time he interviewed her, Paul was insistent on getting into her head, making her have answers for any possible question that may come her way. Just like when studying for an exam, he'd urged, all grounds need to be covered for that perfect score.

Azalea didn't want to ruin her last few memories of her sister alive but Paul went above her and spoke directly to her mother. With all the prep going on, her mother agreed to everything. The second Paul said the defence team would try to say that Hunter was invited to their house by Poppy and that her death was all from a heated loss of control, her mother agreed to any type of question being asked. She knew her mother was trying to protect the memory of Poppy, to ensure that Hunter wouldn't walk free to hurt another, but in Azalea's eyes her mother was just letting the sadist get away with his torturing.

"She told me where she was going. We had no secrets from each other. She was excited to finally see her friends again." Azalea just repeated the lines she'd told him on multiple occasions.

"And was she in contact with the defendant at this time?"

Azalea let a scoff escape. "Would you still be in contact with a man who'd broken your wrist, or who threw you down the stairs for talking to the postman?"

"Miss Hart, please remain serious and answer the question properly."

"No Mr Archer, Poppy was no longer in contact with Hunter. The last time she saw Hunter was before she left him, the day before she found out she was expecting."

"And did Mr Marshall know that your sister was expecting his child? That she was planning to keep his child from him as a secret?"

"No, there is no way he knew."

"Now, Miss Hart, are you absolutely sure there's no way he would have found out this information?"

"I can't say I'm 100% positive, can I?" She huffed. She hated it when he questioned her like this. Like he was trying to force things she didn't know out of her. How would she know if he knew without asking him directly? As far as she knew, no one had told Hunter that Poppy was pregnant. He knew now, of course. It was discussed at length prior to his hearing whether he should be charged with both Poppy's and his unborn child's murder but the courts decided that to charge him with killing a foetus would send the country into a spiral with its' laws regarding abortion. Many people were outraged at him not being charged for both deaths, but it wasn't up to them. The judge ruled supreme and their decision was final.

"Fine, let me rephrase the question. As far as you are aware, did Hunter know that Poppy was expecting his child and her plan to keep him away from the child?"

"No, as far as I was aware, he did not know about Poppy's pregnancy." She rolled her eyes. Was the hour even close to being over yet?

"Now, Azalea, tell me in detail what you saw that night." This was the worst part. Reliving the evening. She wished she could just skip this bit but she knew this was definitely a question that would be asked more than once. She closed her eyes and took a deep breath, preparing the speech in her head. The more it was planned, the less she would get emotional, or so she hoped.

"I think you did well," her mother glanced at her as Azalea focused on the food in front of her. No part of her wanted to eat. "I know you'll do well when you have to give your statement. Poppy will know you're doing her right."

Azalea pushed her food around her plate with her fork. She knew that she had to eat, that she'd starve otherwise, but she couldn't attempt it right now. She couldn't get the thought of Poppy out of her head. Poppy singing off-key in the front room with musicals on the TV. Poppy flicking loose scraps of paper at Azalea's head as they sat across from each other at the kitchen table working on homework. Poppy dressing up all nice to go to a grown-up party with her best friend. All the memories of her sister flooded her mind but the one thought that haunted her was fictional. Poppy sat in a rocking chair, a delicate little being resting in her arms as she rocked, humming a lullaby. Poppy would never get to live out that scenario. There would be no children for Poppy to coo over and swaddle. She wouldn't get woke up for midnight feedings, or have to change stinky nappies. She would never get to wonder why her child was crying. She was no more, and so was the fractional possibility of her having a happy, well-lived life.

The constant reminder sat with Azalea no matter where she went or what she was doing. She'd given up trying to wear her contacts. Every time the thoughts got too much and she cried, the contact was irritating the surface. She couldn't deal with the overflowing amount of emotional pain she was dealing with; she didn't want to be burdened further with physical pain.

She looked up at her mother. Her mother had sat out of all of the interrogation sessions. She wasn't sure her mother would be able to sit through the entire statement. Not without breaking the strong persona of the mother seeking justice. Her mother had stayed so strong but she knew the second the details came out, her mother would break. She hoped her mother would be okay. She couldn't lose another member of her family. The loss was already too much.

"I do love you, you know?" Her mother said abruptly. The words shook her back into reality. It felt like so long since she'd been told that. Had she even heard it since Poppy died?

"I love you too, mum." She whispered, forcing a smile in her mother's direction. With how little she could feel at that time, and how numb she felt to the bone, she wasn't even sure that was true.

I always thought the distance between us

Would be a matter of miles

I never in my life dreamt

That the distance would be

6 feet of ground

Glazed with morning dew

I dreamt of us growing old

With separate lives

So delicately intertwined

That every special moment would be shared

And every heartache conquered together

But those thoughts will forever be

A haunting of what could have been

If you'd lived

Chapter 15

Time seemed to speed by without Tabby to keep her company. The weeks flew by and before she knew it, it was the day she was due to give her statement. Every inch of her being wanted to run away before she was summoned in to speak.

She waited in a separate room, Paul to her right. The room was just as bland as his general presence. She could feel her heart racing. She knew she was being called today but they gave her no particular time. All she knew was she had to wait and that was making it worse.

"You'll do fine," he reassured her which was the weirdest thing to hear coming from his lips, especially after the hours he spent making her relive the nightmare.

"I feel like I'm going to be sick," she murmured, staring at her shaking hands. She didn't want to be there. She wanted to run. Just being this close to Hunter was causing her heart to bruise her ribcage. What if she said the wrong thing? What if they blamed everything on her, just like she always had? What if even with her witness statement the judge still decided to let Hunter go free to beat, bruise and break another innocent person? What if he got out and came after her and her mother?

"Stop overthinking it." Paul urged, as if he was reading her mind. "If it gets hard, if it gets too much and you feel yourself getting emotional, just say so. We're not going to keep you up there if you start to break down."

She nodded her head. Her mouth felt so dry she didn't dare to speak until she was on the stand. She gulped desperately from her bottle of water, hoping it will relieve some of the dryness and nausea.

"Is there anyone you want to speak to, anyone who will calm you down? I can go grab your mother?" Paul questioned.

"No, no. My mum was adamant she wanted to hear every detail in the trial, it wouldn't be fair to pull her away."

"Are you sure? Is there anyone else?"

"There's someone…" Azalea sighed. "But I'm not sure if she'll pick up."

"Well, I'll leave you to your call and I'll wait in the hallway. If you need me, or if they call you in the meantime, I'm just outside."

As puzzled as she was at how Paul was being, she shrugged it off. It was his career after all. He probably wasn't always as hard as he seemed. She hesitated as she flicked through her contacts and found the one person she'd wanted to cry to since the trial had begun. She needed some friendly comfort and if she didn't try and reach out, nothing would happen.

As the phone line rang, she found herself holding her breath. It ringing was a good sign. She expected it to go straight to voicemail. One ring. Two. Three.

"Hello?" A slurred, tired voice yawned down the other end.

"Tabby? It's Az. I know you might not like me, and you might just hang up, but I need a friend right now. It's Hunter." Tears were starting to form in the corners of her eyes and she hastily pushed them away.

She heard Tabby straighten up as objects tumbled to the floor from wherever Tabby was. "What happened? Are you okay?"

"It's the trial. It's my day." She bit her lip hard. As much as she'd wanted to hear Tabby's voice, to have her friend back, she didn't know what to say since the last time she pushed she'd been pushed out.

"Shit! Fuck! Already? Fuck." Tabby sighed heavily. "I'm so, so sorry Az. For how it went down when you were here. I was going to reach out but..." For a moment, it felt like the phone line had gone dead from the silence between the two. "I got bad. I still am bad," she emphasized, "and at that moment, I just wanted to be alone. Part of me still wants that but I was going to reach out before the trial, so you weren't alone coz I know that sucks. I've lived it, I know it's atrocious. Time has just gone faster than I'd thought." The slur in Tabby's voice became more obvious as she rambled.

"Are you drunk?" Azalea questioned, wanting to focus on Tabby more in that instant than what was happening behind a set of double doors in this building somewhere. She felt she could almost smell the liquor on Tabby's breath through the phone.

"Just a little. Helps me cope right now. Don't judge."

"Tabby," Azalea shook her head, pushing that sentence down. She was not going to put any more pressure on her, not now. Not now there was communication.

"Yeah?"

"Nevermind," she sighed, "Just tell me today is going to be okay and that his shithead is going away for an extremely long time."

"Azalea, you've got this. He is going away forever and he will never, ever do what he did to Poppy again." Tabby sounded so confident, it almost reassured Azalea that it was true.

A knock interrupting the little bubble the phone call had created around Azalea. Paul popped his head around the door, a sad smile across his face as he glanced at her.

"Wish me luck," she murmured down the phone to Tabby as she hung up and slid the phone into her pocket. She felt her phone buzz once more and she knew it was Tabby, texting her to remind her it'll be okay.

She felt all the eyes focus on her as she made her way across the front of the room to the witness stand. She took a deep breath, focusing on the echo of her footsteps on the wooden floor. She didn't want to look at him, not yet. She kept her eyes aligned with the chair in front of her and climbed into position as Paul went to take his seat next to Arthur at the prosecutor's table.

As soon as she was sat, Arthur rose to his feet and took the floor like a vulture waiting for a predator to move away from the carcass.

"Good afternoon, Azalea. I hope you are well. Are you ready to answer some questions in front of the court today?" he enquired as he approached the witness stand. He stood tall in the centre of the room, prepared to entertain his on-looking audience.

She looked Arthur in the eyes and nodded. "Yes, sir."

"Can you state your full name for the court."

"Azalea Rose Hart." In her peripheral, she could just make out the jury as they inched closer in their seats to get a better look at her. Their 24 eyes drilled holes into her every inch.

"And what is your relation to the victim?"

"The victim…" The word hung on her tongue, like a slick coat of something bitter, "Poppy," She continued, "was my older sister."

"And where were you on the evening of the 31st October last year?"

"I was sat at home, waiting for trick or treaters to come get sweets with horror movies on. The only time I left the house was when I thought one of our cats had gotten out and that was only for a brief moment."

"And where was Poppy?"

"She was home, but she wasn't supposed to be. She had to change her costume before heading out to her friend's party."

"And why did she have to change her outfit, Miss Hart? Please, tell the jury and Mr Marshall just why Poppy was still home at that point."

Azalea took another deep breath and forced herself to look at him. Hunter looked at her curiously, massive purple bags hanging under his eyes. It was evident from the look on his sunken face that up until this point he hadn't considered her a threat to his not guilty plea.

"Poppy was two months' pregnant and was experiencing a bad case of morning sickness at the time. She'd just accidentally been sick on herself and had to clean herself up before leaving."

"And at that time, did Mr Marshall know your sister was pregnant?"

"He did not. She didn't want him to know. As soon as she found out she was pregnant, she left him that same day." She kept looking at Hunter, waiting for his exterior to crack but everything she said just seemed to make his smile grow. The man sat 20 feet from her, handcuffed and guarded, was a sick man taking pleasure in his own crime.

"So you said earlier that you left to go looking for your cat? Around what time would you say you were out of the house and how long for?"

"Yes," she replied finally looking away from the criminal who was breathing the same air as her. "I left for around 15 minutes to look for Storm. Poppy brought her home when she moved back in to stop Hunter from doing anything to her and we were trying to keep her in to keep her safe since she wasn't used to the area yet." Her glance found her mother in the crowd and she decided to keep her focus there. She had to be strong for her and for Poppy. They all needed this. They needed justice for her death. She swallowed and continued to speak.

"I found her in one of our neighbour's bins and when I came home, the door I left on latch was wide open."

"Please," Arthur urged, "continue with the story."

She nodded, her hands fidgeting on the desk in front of her tapping out the only beat she could think of. "At first, I thought maybe the wind had blown it open. Until I heard her scream and the smash of glass. I could hear the commotion from across the street. I remember cradling Storm to my chest as I ran back in. I dropped her to the floor and shut the door behind me. I could hear Poppy crying and pleading, calling my name. So I moved as fast as I could to find her."

"And what happened when you found her? How was she? Where was she?" Arthur pushed further and she could feel every set of eyes in the room glued to her, as if she was a celebrity posing for the paparazzi.

"She was on the floor, the living room mirror was smashed all around her." She squeezed her eyes shut, as if that would make any difference to the memories flooding through her mind. "When I got in he was kicking her and punching her. She was already so bloody. She was just crying and begging him to stop. That's when she told him she was pregnant, but he didn't stop. It looked like he started to kick her harder."

"And how long was it before he realised you were there?"

"I think he only realised when I tried to pull him away. I didn't know he had a knife in his pocket. Not until he attacked me."

"And what happened then?" She felt like the interrogation was never-ending. She knew she'd be pressed and poked until every detail was out, but no matter how much she'd prepared with Paul the questions were just hard.

"Then he threw me across the room, followed me to where I'd landed and stabbed me in the face a few times, completely damaging my sight in one eye. In the long run, it is not the worst thing that happened that night obviously." Being serious was eating at her, so much so the sarcasm was creeping out. "I passed out for a few minutes and when I woke up, he was gone. I checked the house, rang the police and an ambulance then checked her pulse even though I knew it was pointless. There was blood everywhere, coming from cuts and wounds, and her head looked slightly caved in. Then I just sat there waiting."

She couldn't hold back the tears anymore. It hurt too much. Reliving Poppy's last night killed her mentally and emotionally and she knew deep down she would be reliving it for the rest of her life, no matter what. She couldn't properly grieve until Hunter was locked up and she doubted even then she would be able to.

Arthur approached the stand and handed her a box of tissues. He patted her hands lightly, giving them a slight squeeze. "Thank you for your answers, Miss Hart. That is all I have to ask. Your honour, may I request a brief recess before the cross-examination if that is fine with the defence?"

The judge glanced at the defence barrister who nodded swiftly. "Recess is granted. Court will resume at 1PM sharp." He looked at Azalea solemnly and gave her a faint smile as he left his post to his quarters in the back of the courtroom. Azalea looked down at the tissue in her hand and sighed. She knew the worst part wasn't over yet.

She sat in the seat once more as the defence barristers shuffled the papers on his desk. The man and woman duo whispered to each other, clearly getting their plan clear before the woman coughed lightly into her hand, neatened her papers and rose to her feet.

"Miss Hart, thank you for participating with this trial. I know it is hard to recount your own experiences. Believe me, we won't make you repeat them much longer. We just have a few more questions." The woman smiled her way, but it never reached her eyes. "Are you okay if we go ahead with asking?"

Azalea glanced from the judge to the prosecution team. Paul nodded lightly at her. "Yes, I'm ready." She took a deep breath, and made eye contact with each of the jury members before exhaling. Once she exhaled, she found the dead eyes of her mother in the gallery and smiled patiently. "Please, go ahead."

"Prior to the evening in question, were you a witness to any abuse from Mr Marshall towards your sister?"

"No, prior to that evening I'd never seen him physically abuse her. I did notice verbal and emotional abuse though."

"What do you mean by verbal and emotional abuse?" The defence questioned, looking at her client. The look on her face made it obvious that Hunter had never mentioned that she'd be present more than once when this had happened.

"He threatened her. He isolated her. He said he'd kill her then himself if she ever left him."

Her last words fuelled anger in the defence barrister's eyes. At least she couldn't dig Hunter out of his own mess if he'd ignored it had ever happened.

"I see," the defence murmured, looking at her partner at the table, "I have no further questions." She coughed lightly into her hands once more. "Derrick?" She pleaded. Her colleague just shook his head. Any questions they had clearly relied on it being a one-off episode. Now it was evident it wasn't, all questions were out the window. She straightened herself and headed back to the defence table as the man named Derrick slumped into his hands. "No further questions, your honour."

The judge turned to Azalea and frailly smiled. "Thank you for your statement, Miss Hart. You may now leave the witness stand." Azalea hurried to her feet and rushed from the room at the side of the usher. As she left, she glanced at the defence team. Their whispering now was angry in tone and they both kept glaring at Hunter, who was looking at the courtroom clock, avoiding every watching eye. Hopefully, she prayed, that meant things would go her way.

Chapter 16

By the 24th August, the jurors had heard and seen all the evidence, listened to all the statements and been advised by the judge about juror procedure. As they left to deliberate, Azalea squeezed her mother's hand hard. Since giving her statement, she'd spent every day of the trial sat next to her mother, her bag and pockets padded with tissues, mints and refreshments. The gallery members started to fumble around, leaving the courtroom. She remained still, waiting to see what her mother wanted to do. They knew it could take from mere hours to weeks for the jury to decide their verdict, but Azalea knew her mother wouldn't move far from the room. She wouldn't leave the court until she'd been given an answer and the furthest she would go was their hotel room across the road.

"Want to wait here, or wait for the call?" Azalea questioned her mother as the room became empty aside from themselves. The prosecutors had promised they'd call as soon as the jurors were ready to announce their verdict. Her mother remained as silent as she'd been for days but rose to her feet.

Azalea followed her to the local café, just around the corner from the courthouse, where her mother ordered a black coffee and sat barely sipping the drink, her phone on the table, her hand lightly tapping the table's surface next to it. Azalea ordered herself a drink, and continued to order more as every beverage was finished, her mother's fingertips still tapping, waiting for the phone to ring.

Her mother was on her 4th black coffee when the phone finally rang. Either the verdict was quick, or someone was being extremely inconsiderate when they knew what was going on in the life of the Harts. The number appeared as unknown and her mother hesitated to answer. Swooping in, Azalea grabbed the phone from the table and let out a deep breath.

"H-h-hello?" She stammered to the other end of the line.

"Azalea," Paul responded, "Is your mother available?" Azalea handed the phone to her mother, who rose to her feet and walked outside before starting to speak. Azalea sipped her tea as her mother paced on the pavement, lips moving too fast to read. She hoped her mother would return soon and update her but it was another 15 minutes until she returned to the table.

"It's time to go back," her mother sighed, "they've reached a verdict." As much as they both knew this verdict was needed, something was needed to justify Poppy's death, it had come too fast. Azalea was hesitant. She knew it could go either way, dependant on her the jury were feeling that day towards Hunter.

She wasn't present to hear his own statement, but from what Paul had told her after her statement was finished, he was quite charismatic on the stand. That was enough to put doubt in her mind.

Making their way back to the courtroom, her mother remained in silence. Azalea knew her mother was probably as nervous as she was. There was no guarantee that the jury would swing to the prosecution, even if all the evidence presented showed just how guilty Hunter was. All they could do was wish that Hunter would be found guilty and would rot in prison for the rest of his life.

As the room settled around them, her eyes drifted to the back of Hunter's head. She could see the cockiness steaming off him. He glanced around the room himself, a smile stretched across his face, as if he were the cat who got the cream. He found the Harts in the crowd and his grin stretched further. He winked in their direction before blowing a kiss at Azalea. Her stomach turned. Just how could he act like that? The anger was brewing inside her and all she wanted to do was cause him more pain than he'd ever caused her.

They all rose as the judge entered the room and it felt like only moments later that the jury were back on their bench, ready to deliver their verdict.

"Jurors, have you reached a verdict?" The judge questioned as everyone intently watched them.

"We have, your honour," the head juror replied.

"And what is your verdict?" The judge pressed.

"We find the defendant guilty of premeditated murder, your honour," he announced to the room. There was a burst of noise as the gallery responded to the verdict. Azalea turned to her mother and saw that the tears that streamed down her own face were matched. She wrapped an arm around her mother and lightly pressed her lips into her mother's hair. She just hoped that the sentence was a long enough one.

The crowds were urged to quieten as the judge prepared to sentence Hunter. You could tell by Hunter's body language, even from behind, that the smug smile had been wiped from his face. His charm had won him no favour with the general public.

"Due to the nature of the crime, Mr Marshall," the judge ruled, "and the verdict provided by a jury of your peers which came back justifiably fast, I must sentence you as appropriate. This crime which you initially declared you were not involved with, to which your statement changed later to it being a crime of passion, had clear evidence of the opposite. With the crime being clearly premeditated, evidenced by the knife you brought to the house of the Harts on that evening, and the prior abuse towards the victim, the evidence of which has been provided throughout this trial from photographed bruises and witness statements from multiple individuals, I feel these aggravating factors should be taken into your sentence. I sentence you to a minimum of 25 years before you can appeal to the parole board."

The judge found Azalea's face in the gallery and smiled sadly. "Unfortunately for the family of Poppy Hart, your sentence will not bring their daughter and sister back. It will not bring back the bundle of life that Poppy was expecting, or the opportunities she could have had. We will never know if this young woman would have been a good mother, or if she ever had a chance of succeeding in the life you took from her."

The judge's eyes then focused on Hunter. "I can only hope, Mr Marshall, that you become remorseful in the next 25 years and that you never forget just what you have done to an expectant young woman who sadly loved you too much." The judge stood high and waved to the courtroom. "Court dismissed. Please guards, escort Mr Marshall back to his cell to prepare for his return to his new home." He glanced at Azalea and her mother once more and nodded before leaving the room.

Azalea rose to her own feet and grabbed her mother's hand, dragging her out into the hallway of the court building. She continued to pull her mother with her until they got outside. As the cold air hit them, they were approached by a few reporters. Azalea shook her head and whispered lightly to her mother. "No statements, just walk." Her mother nodded in response. They ignored the reporters who raised microphones and recorders in their direction.

"No comment," Azalea called to them all repeatedly as she pushed her mother through until they reached the hotel. Thankfully now they could return home to their own beds and the comfort of the cats. Whilst Azalea knew they probably would never feel as comfortable as they could in that house, she also knew they couldn't leave. That home was theirs, no one else's. Poppy had lived there, and that is where they wanted to stay.

Chapter 17

Even being back in contact with Azalea, things with Tabby hadn't improved. She was glad things had started to look up for her friend, but she also knew hers was on the verge of hitting rock bottom. She'd just had to end her fling with Laine. She was getting too paranoid for her own safety, never mind the safety of someone else. She was just glad that she'd kept it practically silent. His name wasn't mentioned to friends, it wasn't typed in text, and it wasn't even spoken unless she was speaking directly to him. She had to keep him as a ghost, just in case. She hoped he understood why, but she doubted it.

But now, even if he didn't, it was too dangerous. Too dangerous to have friends. Too dangerous to have pets. Too dangerous to even fancy a sweet guy who had never done anything wrong in his life. Laine could have been good for her. Ah well, she sighed, it was over now. She couldn't keep it going now. He'd be dead if he'd stayed active in her life.

It wasn't long after her call to her grandfather's new home, to check he'd settled in well, that she received the call from an unknown number. She knew she'd have to answer it, even if she regretted it. It could be the police. It could be the solicitors. It could be him. It could be anyone.

"Tabitha?" the voice on the other end of the line asked. Lucy. Thank god. She let out an initial sigh of relief before responding.

"Hey Lucy, yeah it's me."

"Hey," Lucy hesitantly responded. Just from her voice, Tabby could tell she'd wanted it to go to voicemail so she had more time to prepare for this conversation.

"It's about him, isn't it?" Tabby inhaled deeply and held it for a moment before exhaling. She wanted to stay as calm as possible.

From the hesitation in Lucy's voice, the point of this call became more obvious. "He's being freed, isn't he?" Tabby beat Lucy to the punch. She didn't want this call to last for longer than it had to because her legal team were dragging their feet in how to tell her bad news.

"Tabitha, if you want to come down to the office to discuss it more or if you want us to come to you, we can get that arranged."

"When is he out?" She cut to the point. There was no point dawdling around. She didn't need to know much. Just when.

There was a loud sigh at the other end of the phone line before she heard Lucy reply. "He's out at the end of the month."

"Thank you for the call. Goodbye." Tabby's response was so autonomous but she didn't know how to feel. She was supposed to have longer to process everything, but the damned legal system took that away from her.

She tossed her phone at the lounge chair, as far away from her as possible. She didn't want to deal with anyone else today. She had to get out of the flat and breathe. She grabbed the essentials, minus her phone, and ran as if the devil himself was chasing her.

As she crawled up the staircase to her floor, not trusting her legs to stand straight or climb properly, Tabby dared to think. She'd spent the evening shutting her brain down as much as she could, but a stray thought brought her back to a sobering reality. He couldn't kill her if she was already dead.

It had been a long time since she last thought that way. That she'd be better off dead and buried than alive. She'd promised herself, more than once, that she'd ignore the thoughts if they ever came back but this time, they seemed completely logical. She had nothing to live for. Not really. She was completely isolated. Her only living relative had to move away due to their own health. Her only true friends existed primarily through a screen. She had no job and survived on the minimal government handouts, aside from the inheritance she'd saved for a rainy day. £5000, waiting for the inevitable worsts that could occur in day to day life.

Would anyone even notice, she pondered to herself. How long would it be before someone came searching? Easily a few weeks, if not months. Her rent was automatically taken from her bank account so as long as she had money, the landlord wouldn't come knocking and she still had a reasonable amount in her savings account to keep that going for a while.

She tried to shake the thoughts out of her mind, but the wheels were already turning. She finally found her landing and attempted to stand as she unlocked her door. No, she wouldn't die. Not yet. It was just the alcohol feasting on her depression trying to encourage her. While the wheels turned, she focused on reassuring herself. Sobering her mind, but not her body. She still had a few things to live for. It might not be a lot, but it was something.

Tripping into the doorframe, she cursed herself. Was the hand she had been given by the universe really worth living for? No matter how hard she tried to think of other things, her thoughts kept slipping to how easy it would be. A slice into a main artery. A rope to hang from. A bottle of booze and pills, mixed into a bitter concoction. A gas tap left leaking and an open flame. A little fly from the top floor of a tower block.

No, she thought, she couldn't. It couldn't be that easy. It couldn't be that simple. As little as her life meant to her, it couldn't be as easy as taking a handful of pills. She triumphantly managed to open the door to her flat, the door swinging open and bouncing against the wall with a loud thud.

An even louder, exasperated sigh escaped her dry lips. Even if he wasn't in her life, even if she never saw him again, part of Tabby knew she could never escape him. The one time she thought she had, the one time she thought she was truly free, ended in complete disaster.

It all seemed to happen so fast. One minute he was slapping her and pushing her against the wall, arms pinned above her head with his right hand as he sneered and spread her legs roughly. The next he was sprawled, clutching his manhood and whimpering, whilst her left knee hovered in the air. She'd finally had enough of him. She saw her chance to flee and she had to take it. She didn't know why this was the time that pushed her to leave, to fight dirty for the chance, but it was an opportunity here to take. Grabbing her phone, keys and bag she sprang out the door.

She ran for her life. She didn't turn back, not even when she could hear the plodding of his heavy footsteps on her tail. Thankfully her small stature gave her an advantage and she was able to create some distance and hide from him, squeezed behind a dumpster holding her breath. She held it for as long as she could, the rotting refuge filling her nose with the foulest of odours. When it seemed he had finally disappeared out of view, she shuffled her way from behind the stinky steel tin and took in a deep breath.

"I'm never going back," she whispered to herself, promising as wholeheartedly as her fragile heart could, "not to him."

Unfortunately, there weren't many options for where she could go. Her grandfather's care home had strict rules for families and she doubted she could hide from their staff until she got her shit together. She could try a women's shelter, but at this time of night she knew she'd never get a bed. It was moments like these that she wished that she had more family and friends, but as an orphan she had no one blood-related to persuade to open their doors and any friends she did have had been long since abandoned when he came into the picture.

She cursed herself for letting him have so much control. She'd always believed she was a strong, independent woman, but he'd made her feel like she was worth less than the shit on the paving stones outside his flat. Even though she'd lived there for nearly as long as they'd been together, she'd never considered it her home. It was always his. Everything in there was his. Her belongings weren't allowed and even her essential woman products were hidden away from the world, as if they'd ever have visitors.

She tried not to think about it, but her mind reminded her of the good old days, when they'd first started out. When he was loving. Attentive. She was the only thing in his life. He was sober, hard-working. She'd been warned by everyone who ever glanced his way that he was trouble, but she didn't see it. The red flag was hidden behind her rose-tinted, insanely-in-love sunglasses, preventing her from seeing the truth.

It wasn't long before his true colours started to flow into her reality. His romantic tendencies were the first walls to fall. Every moment she'd gushed to her friends about, while she still had friends, fluttered from existence. No more bouquets of roses just because, no more bubble baths and a glass of wine waiting after work. Bit by bit, his charade crumbled until all she could see was the evil man that lay beneath.

Instead of immense conversations after work, she was now greeted by his boozy breath and drug habits. It was only a matter of weeks before he was making her do the drugs alongside him. Why, he often questioned, would she want to be sober while he was enjoying the high life? He claimed that he wanted to experience things with her, but she knew differently. He wanted her addicted, reliant, needy. He wanted her to a point where she could not survive without his very presence. A handful of cuts and bruises later, and attempts to jab her veins as she fought, she gave in. She couldn't fight him off forever and at least they eased some of the pain for a time.

Once the drugs started to increase in frequency, so did his paranoia. No more friends. No more job. If she wanted to go anywhere, he should be there too. She couldn't inhale the same air as another man as far as he had a say. If she did, there would be a price to pay. A black eye, maybe, or a broken rib. A&E became a home away from home, but she still returned. She loved him, foolishly, with all of her being no matter what he did to her. For months and months, she dealt with the hits. She dealt with the physical, sexual, emotional and mental abuse he chucked her way.

She agreed with the words he threw at her. She was worthless. She was a slut, a whore, an overly-used sex toy on the verge of falling apart. Who else would want someone so fucked that there was sex workers with lower tallies? She was ugly, fat, hideous. No one with any sense would want to be with her, or would even want to be around her for too long. As the poison rolled heavily off his tongue, it seeped into her heart and head, tainting every thought she could ever have. He told her time and time again that she was worthless, not worth the effort of anyone. The only people who'd touch a whore like her were junkies and dealers, and he made sure of that. Every time he was low on cash, or he was offered free gear for a ride, her body was on the table. It didn't matter if she said no; it didn't matter if she fought; it didn't matter if she cried – she could tell that sometimes the sick perverts who raped her repeatedly preferred it that way. Their pleasure came from seeing her scared. Not that any of it mattered to him. Her body was up for sale to the highest bidder when he could score. He cared more about the heroin than he did about her. She cried for the man he once was, but she knew he was never going to come back. Now she'd seen the man behind the mask, there was no way she would be able to see the kind side he had once shown her. Over time, she just accepted the life that was given to her. She wouldn't waste her energy on fighting the inevitable.

She would have never seen the light out of the darkness, if it hadn't have been for her greatest mistake and blessing wrapped in one tiny, human-shaped bundle. She fell pregnant. It wasn't intentional, it wasn't planned and it definitely came from being raped, but from the moment she found out, she had never loved anything as much. Unfortunately, her love for her unborn child is what drove him too far, too far beyond her breaking point.

The moment those two words left her lips, he turned into a beast she had never seen before. His eyes filled with fury whilst his hands turned into fists. Hit after hit, he punched her in her stomach screaming down at her as he knocked her to the floor, cradling her stomach.

"It's not mine, you fuck!" He yowled, starting to kick her hard instead "You cheating bitch, fucking die!"

He pushed her against the wall, continuing to hit and kick and shriek until he ran out of energy. Once his rage had ran out, he turned to the heroin. As he made his way to the bedroom to shoot up, Tabby's head started spinning and she felt herself slip from there. She woke to find herself in a pool of blood. An attendance at A&E with an emergency scan confirmed it, she'd lost her baby and sustained a fair amount of damage to her uterus. When they asked her how it happened, all she could muster was the lie she'd repeated on a dozen of occasions before.

"I fell down the stairs."

Stood around thinking in the blistering cold, she had to fight the urge to go back to the toasty flat. She started to walk, hoping to find somewhere warm and open at this time. She had some coins in her bag, though she had no idea how much. Since she'd started planning for an escape, she scrounged together every penny she could find that he didn't seem to notice. With him being in control of both of their money, including the benefits she received for no longer working, every single pence had to be accounted for, but the loose change he'd accidentally dropped in the flat was fair game. When he was at work, she'd search the cushions and floors, grasping at every slither of silver or cooper on the hard wooden floors.

She walked the footpaths until she finally saw the neon words of her dreams. She should have expected that the most popular fast food franchise was open 24/7. Approaching the till, she counted the shrapnel she'd pulled out of her bag. A few pounds and pennies, enough for a bite to eat and a boiling hot black coffee. Thanking the server, she took her things and sat at a table in the corner. Finally alone, with some warmth from the elements, she found herself crying. She had nowhere to turn and no one to fall back on. All she could do was hope there was still money in the account her grandfather had started for her, a secret she'd kept safely tucked away from him this whole time. She couldn't imagine her inheritance going towards their drug habit. It was all she had left from her parents. That and a photo she may never get back from the flat she fled from. The tears were falling thicker, flooding her cheeks, glistening under the florescent lights as she thought of all her sacred memories, abandoned in a box buried in a cupboard.

Raising the steaming cup to her lips, she winced from the heat. Everything hurt. Withdrawals were hitting harder than she could ever have imagined, but she had to persevere. Cold turkey. No him. No heroin. The track marks were healing and she wanted them to stay that way. She couldn't stay hooked to that toxicity any longer.

A few hours later, and after a free refill courtesy of the kind server who saw her distress, Tabby was prepared to brace the world once more. With the few belongings she had on her shoved in her bag, she started to head to her grandfather's care home. She'd speak to her grandfather, rummaging through his documents if necessary, to see if she had enough financial padding to keep her safe for a while longer before seeing if any of the city's many women's shelters had any room for a few nights.

She wasn't far from the care home when it happened. It couldn't have been more than 3 or 4 o'clock. She felt it before she even saw him. The liquid tossed terribly at her face, missing entirely followed by a rapidly-burning sensation to her scalp. He'd clearly been lying in wait with the acid, knowing she'd eventually go to the only person she had left in the world that wasn't him, ready to pounce. She turned and saw the darkness in his eyes staring back at her as he started to punch her. Once. Twice. Thrice. She screamed and she pleaded for help of any kind and though it may have only been a few seconds, it felt like an eternity until he was running away as a group of students ran to her side. An ambulance was called but it didn't matter to her whether or not they made it. All she wanted was for the pain to take her away.

She spent a week and a half in intensive care, feeling like a prisoner under lock and key with tubes coming out of her and a police escort hovering at the door. She was lucky, the doctors repeatedly remarked. That his aim was so bad. That the sulphuric acid missed her face entirely, only damaging her scalp and the back of her neck. That the worst of the damage could easily be hidden away under wigs or hats.

Between the doctors and the police, who struggled to find him for 5 days after the attack, she had never felt any more alone. She had no one to hold her hand and tell her he was going away now for a long time. She had no one to promise her that life would get better, that it was worth living and that she should be grateful to be alive. She had no one to help her out of the hospital, or to hide her away from the gasps and shocked expressions of the general public. She wished she had just died and that everything would just leave her be, but she had no luck. She was still stuck alive, even if she didn't want to be.

Before she knew it, the plan was forming on the cusp of her thoughts. They'd been there before, but never as vivid as this. Never as calculated. Never as planned and thorough, down to a T. It couldn't be messy. She had to be the perfect corpse for whoever found her. No blood, no gore. It couldn't cause the death of others unjustly, so no fire or explosion. One strike of a match and the entire building could go up in smoke. With how unstable she was on her feet, she doubted she'd be capable enough to tie a noose and hang it for her body to dangle from so that option was out, as was a jump from the roof which was likely locked anyway. That left her with only one option. Pills and alcohol.

Haphazardly stumbling, she carried herself and the bottles of vodka she had purchased on her way home to the bathroom. She knew she had some painkillers left somewhere for in case of an emergency and her antidepressants were doing her no good, sitting unused in their packets. She fiddled through the medicine cabinet, yanking medication sleeves left and right.

"How many would be enough?" she questioned herself aloud before scoffing. "I'll just take all I can." She nodded to herself in response.

She stumbled through to the bedroom, pills and vodka in hand, grabbing her phone, a notepad and pen on the way. She glanced half-heartedly at the screen. No new messages. No surprise there. She took a glance at her other hand. Half a dozen sleeves of a prescription cocktail should get her on her merry way. Kicking her shoes to the floor, she got herself comfortable. She didn't want to kill herself while not feeling comfortable. That was not the way to do it. She perched herself up in the centre of the bed and struggled to uncap the vodka. With a grunt and a sore hand, she had it removed. One by one, she slowly popped the pills onto her bedspread. 14 slowly turned to 28, then 42, increasing in number until it finally hit 84. Luckily, she thought, all the sleeves were full.

"That's definitely enough," she snorted to herself.

For the first time in her life, in a long time at least, she felt happy. Happy with the decision she was making. Her last act of defiance. She could imagine the look on his face when he found out. For so long, he'd controlled her, made her do everything his way or she'd face the consequences. Even without him physically there, grasping her wrists or stabbing her torso with cigarettes, his voice lived on in her twisted head. Nothing had given her the peace and the silence she'd dreamt of but this could be it. She could finally truly escape him for good. She'd no longer look in the mirror and see his handiwork, or have a bad day being followed by his repulsive attitude. It might not be the way out that she'd dreamt of all those nights she cowered in fear, but now that fear was gone. All she felt was a delirium of happiness flooding her from all directions.

Staring at the notepad she'd brought with her, the words she wanted to write escaped her mind. How could she sum up her final choice to whoever was unfortunate enough to find her? She could be blunt. "My life was shit and I didn't want to live it anymore." She could be apologetic. "I'm sorry I did this, but I felt I had no other choice." She could be detailed. "Rape and domestic violence can kill a girl even when she's out of their reach."

No, she thought to herself, the note would be simple. To the point, but also somewhat understanding. She smirked a little. She couldn't be professional in life, but she could be in death. Delicately, she twirled the pen in her hands, the words flowing out of her. She didn't hold back, she let it all escape her. Once her thoughts had finally ran dry, she placed the pen and pad on her bed. She didn't need them now.

A quick tap of her fingertips on her phone and music filled all the empty air in the room. She kept it low, not to anger or disturb any neighbours. All she needed right now was someone interrupting this final important moment. The flourishes of the piano keys filled the room as Tabby quickly swallowed a pill, and another, and another, an occasional swig of vodka between pills.

She felt the wave of tiredness hit her with half a bottle gone and at least 60 pills in her system. Her eyes started to droop, so she arranged herself comfily in her pillows. A yawn burst out of her lips as she felt them pull into a smile. As her breathing got lighter and her muscles heavier, she couldn't think of anything aside from how happy and at peace she was in that moment. Her eyes clung to the painted phoenix she could see beyond her bedroom door as the world went dark for the last time.

The worst pain

Is the pain of losing you

And not knowing you're gone

Not knowing that you needed me

And that I could have been there

To catch you when you fell

The worst pain is my heart breaking

Because I couldn't save you

From your worst enemy

Yourself

The worst pain is knowing

That now all I can do

Is live without you

And I need to accept that

Because if I don't

I might as well be dead too

Chapter 18

It felt weird. She hadn't had a text in what felt like years. She thought she and Tabby had worked it out. They'd been speaking again. Tabby had been there for her when she needed her the most, but now it felt like she'd pulled away.

Azalea sighed. Maybe Tabby was still dealing with stuff. She'd give her time if she needed it. They had all the time in the world to bask in each other's company. She just wished they'd gotten more of the summer together. After nearly a year of contemplation, and her school offering her a repeat of her previous year with no negative effects to her record due to what they loved to call "exceptional circumstances", she'd finally decided to return to the educational part of her life. Before Poppy's death, she had no idea what she wanted to do but now, though she wasn't much wiser, she knew she wanted to help and finishing college would at least be a step in the right direction. It would all be a fresh start, starting college all over again and maybe, with the help of a guidance counsellor and some lecturers along the way, she could get to a point where she could do some good.

She glared at her phone again. All she wanted to do was share this news with Tabby. Other than her mum, who'd finally started becoming herself some more, she didn't really have anyone to tell. She didn't have many people to begin with and everything that happened just had people dropping off her radar left and right, even the most casual of acquaintances, until she had no one left but a parent and a headstone.

Just thinking of Poppy had her remembering, but now the thoughts had shifted. When she felt the longing for her sister in her heart, her head no longer jumped to the tragic last moments they spent together. Now her mind jumped to thoughts of them as children, joint birthday parties and summer holidays where they sat up all night giggling, sharing secrets. To Azalea, Poppy was never just a sister, she was her best friend and confidante. She told her everything. Every thought, every dream, every crush. She knew Poppy would never tell a soul, no matter how juicy the secret was. It was between them, until death did they part.

Missing Poppy like crazy, she felt an urge she could not shake. She threw on the nearest clothes and shoes and headed for the front door. She felt no need to go through all the usual grooming techniques today and there was no need for her contacts. The only person she wanted to see would never judge her for how she looked. With all the necessities in tow, she decided it was the best time to pay her sister a visit.

Opening the door wide, the cool autumn air breeze swept over her, whipping her hair into a frenzy. Though it was only mid-

September, the seasons were changing fast and before long the leaves would be lay orange and crisp on the pavement, waiting to be crunched below toes whilst children rummage amongst them searching for conkers. Autumn had always been Azalea's favourite time of year. The start of the warm jumper season and an excuse to have hot chocolate when she got in from the cool outdoors. The quick change when the cool weather finally became the snowy season, glazing the world in an icy coat. For the first time in her life though, Azalea wasn't excited about the seasonal change. The change brought Halloween closer and with that the anniversary of the worst day of her life. Her favourite holiday of the year had been tainted and she knew at the bottom of her heart she would never be able to enjoy it again, no matter how long had passed. It could be a year, a decade, a quarter of a century. Halloween would never be the same again.

The wind welcomed her happily into the cemetery, swinging the gates at her very presence as she reached the entrance. Though it was so tightly associated with death, Azalea always found the place peaceful. The quiet. The repetitive colours from the black and grey headstones. The life that still flowed through the land of the dead in the form of pretty bushes and tiny critters, fleeing her footsteps.

By the time she'd reached Poppy's grave, she realised it had been longer than she thought since she last visited. The flowers wilted beyond recognition, the bird droppings that seemed perfectly aimed at the top. Pulling the packet of wipes she'd stowed in her big coat pocket for such an occasion, she wiped down the headstone swiftly. It was unusual, being her age and carrying tools to clean what was essentially a bit of rock. Once Poppy's name sparkled once more and the smile in her photo gleamed, Azalea sat at the base of the stone.

"Hey, sis," she said aloud, "I'm really missing you today." She stared at Poppy's smiling face looking back at her.

"I am finally going back to college," she continued, knowing that there was no point waiting for a response. "I know if you were here, you'd be happy for me. You'd be pissed I stopped going too." She found herself chuckling as more thoughts sprung to mind. Poppy dragging her out of bed when she was faking period pains because their mother believed you should trust everything your children say, no matter what, exclaiming that school was too important to miss even a day of. Poppy was her mother for all essential purposes where their own mother failed to be what other families often referred to as a proper parent.

"I'm just feeling lonely," she went on, "because my life is moving on and the only people I want to talk to are MIA or dead. I'm scared and I feel like I'm a child when I say this but I still want you holding my hand along the way." She rested her head and back against the stone, her body starting to feel heavy as the cold air made her shudder. "I want to help people like you, Pop, and I need you guiding my way. Telling me I can do it, like you used to before every test. I need that faith you had in me."

Azalea looked at the branches of the trees nearby as they swung to and fro. "I wish I had the faith you had in me. All I see when I look in the mirror is shit." She whispered to the wind in a sigh. She shook her head, trying to shake the negative thoughts before they nested.

"Anyway," she carried on, "How's Heaven? If it exists I mean. If it does, I assume you're there. You never did anything wrong in your life. You were such a goody goody golden bollocks when you wanted to be." She smirked, more memories of Poppy flooding her mind. Poppy sweet-talking parents and children alike. Everyone loved her. Everyone except...

"No, I won't think of him." She reassured herself aloud. He did not deserve even a millisecond longer in Poppy's presence, even as a thought. "You are more important."

For what felt like hours, Azalea stayed by Poppy's grave, occasionally inputting some meaningless conversation. She knew, no matter how long she sat there, Poppy would never respond but she felt so at peace just being by her. She would have stayed there all day and night if the clouds hadn't burst, filling the sky with fog and rain. Heading home, she felt a little happier. Poppy may be gone, but she knew she could always turn to her when she needs her the most, even if it was just to listen. Pulling her hood over her head, she raced home to the warmth.

Even though being with Poppy had momentarily calmed her, the weird feeling crept back. After three weeks of no contact from Tabby, she felt there was nothing else she could do. She felt a pit in her stomach and it wouldn't disappear until she heard Tabby's voice. She wasn't picking up the phone and it was going straight to voicemail, so Azalea chose the next best option.

"I'm going to see Tabby," Azalea mentioned one evening over tea to her mother. Her mother looked up at her as if she were crazy — well, crazier than usual. Azalea dropped her gaze. Her mother made her feel insane but even then, sat safely at home, the pit just felt wider as time went on and she couldn't help but worry more. She needed it to stop before it engulfed her completely, inside out.

"But you said you've not heard from her?" Her mother questioned, placing her knife and fork on the plate, fully invested in the conversation.

"Mum," Azalea took a deep breath before she spoke again, preparing for a lot of arguing. "I think something is wrong. I feel it in my stomach. Her phone's going straight to voicemail and that's not normal. I need to make sure she's okay." She braced for the fight to come. It could easily go all night, knowing her mother's track record in the last year.

Her mother just nodded. Azalea was stunned. It wasn't the response she was expecting. She was expecting to be told no repeatedly, almost as if it was recorded on a loop.

"Fine, but I'm going with you." Azalea smiled. Even with a compromise, she was getting her way and at least this way she would get to check on Tabby without her mother harassing her every moment she was gone. Her mother might even pay for the train tickets. Her smile was short-lived, as the feeling of dread grew in her stomach. She just hoped everything with Tabby was okay.

Chapter 19

The journey didn't feel as long as Azalea remembered, but maybe the loneliness increased it for her the first time around. Sitting here with her mother, she felt slightly odd. Her and Tabby had only met outside of the camping experience twice and now here she was, dragging her mother alongside her. She knew she needed to re-bond with her mother, but she never assumed it would be in the form of a potential rescue mission.

"Are you okay?" Her mother asked, placing her hand on her knee and squeezing. Looking into her mother's eyes she could see the sadness buried deep. Her mother was worried, more worried than she'd ever been, and she knew exactly why. Her mother was scared for her. Azalea had already lost a sister, she didn't need to lose her new friend too. Her mother knew how close she was to the edge, already dangling to the abyss, that even the slightest change might push her.

She nodded. She couldn't form words at that moment. Dread was eating at part of her. The last time someone she loved went silent, it was because she was buried in the ground. She didn't want to see Tabby like that. She didn't want to even think of that as a possibility, but she couldn't think of any other reason. She knew herself just how bad depression could be, and she knew Tabby was in a bad way, but she never thought it was that bad.

She regretted leaving her when she did. She should have stayed. She should have fought harder. She should have locked her and Tabby in the flat and talked it out. Until Tabby was calm. Until she was okay. Until whatever darkness that was lingering around her had dissipated. She tried to shake the thoughts out of her head discreetly, not wanting to upset her mother further. Her mother didn't need any more worry on her plate and it was globally known that hindsight is a bitch.

Part of her hated herself so much. She may not have been the person who destroyed her family, but she was the one who seemed to be constantly getting in the way of the healing process and the one opening old wounds, peeling away the scabs until it bled once more. Looking at her mother out of the corner of her good eye, she wished she could be someone else. Someone her mother didn't need to constantly fret over. Someone mentally fit enough to cope on her own, without her mother holding her hand every step of the way. She had to be strong, even if it was hard and felt fruitless. She couldn't let her own demons stop her mother from living her life. Taking her mother's hand in her own, she squeezed it tight.

More than anything, she wished she could go back. A year. Five. Ten. Her entire lifetime. If she could go back, she'd try harder. She'd try to be a daughter her mother could be proud of. Outgoing and social, so her mother didn't need to worry how she'd be if one of her friends disappeared every once in a while because she could make more. Brave, not scared of the shadows creeping in the night. Smart and thoughtful, considerate, happy. If she could go back, she'd change it all. She'd be a mini Poppy if that's what her mother needed. She'd be perfect if it meant her mother never had to worry again.

Poppy. Now the thoughts were there, she couldn't shake them. She missed her badly. How many months had it been, since she'd seen her smile? Since her laugh had echoed the four walls of her bedroom? Too long, Azalea sighed away the thoughts. It had been far too long. She tried to think about the happy memories she shared with Poppy but she was grasping at straws. Most of her thoughts were clouded by her death. Maybe her mother could help. Maybe her mother could remember what her mind was blocking out. She needed those smiles, those giggles, those moments of greatness with the only sister she would ever have. She didn't want the only memories of her sister to be from the night of the murder. That was in the past and nothing could change that. She just hoped the other memories were just hidden for now and not lost forever, buried under all the bad thoughts and memories that regularly surfaced.

"Mum?" She asked, "Can you tell me some stories about Poppy when she was younger?" A faint smile crossed her mother's lips.

"You never want to hear about the old days," her mother gushed, "are you sure?"

Azalea smiled. "Please," she pleaded, "I want to remember."

"Okay, is there anything you want to know in particular?" Her mother couldn't help it. Her grin was almost spreading ear to ear. Azalea was happy she could still make her mother smile, after all this time.

It wasn't long before the train pulled into the station. Looping her mother's arm in her own, she pulled up the map on her phone. Typing in the postcode, she waited for the app to load. Five miles. Not that far.

"We can walk it, if you want?" Her mother asks.

Before she can hold it, a scoff escapes her lips. "Mum, have you ever seen me walk more than 10 feet?"

"True, I think I briefly believed I actually had a healthy child." A grin snuck onto her mother's face. She squeezed Azalea's bicep and dragged her a little. "Come on, there's got to be a taxi rank around here somewhere."

Azalea let herself be pulled. Part of her was hesitant. She could feel it deep in her stomach. Something wasn't right. She felt like a lamb heading into the slaughter. She has no idea what to expect when she knocked on the flat's door. She knew Tabby had substance issues, could she be using again? Would she be unconscious on the couch, or completely irrationally delusional? Would she even be there, or would she be huddled in a crack den somewhere, shooting up more than her fill? Azalea hated the path her mind was taking her down, but she couldn't stop it. She didn't know what was going to be hidden, waiting to be disturbed, behind the thin wooden pane that Tabby called her front door.

As her mother continued to pull her, she took in her surroundings. The bustlers, hassling the passer-bys for change nearly as much as the overwhelming homeless population that haunted the city's main streets. The heavy foot traffic, people too busy to breathe as they hastily sped from A to B, ignoring all in between the two points. The litter, caking every possible surface.

Beer cans crumbled and trodden, gum gripping to the bottom of the passing shoes.

The constant movement was overbearing. She could feel her anxiety building up inside of her as people pressed and pushed, trying to work their way around the breathing obstruction that she had become. She stopped for a second and took a deep breath. She could do this. She wasn't doing it for her, she was doing it for Tabby. Looking forward, she found her mother also stopped, a worried expression on her face. With a nod to her mother, they continued, working their way through the crowds until they'd finally made it to the taxi bay.

Giving the driver the postcode, Azalea and her mother crawled into the back of the black cab, their bags flung to the floor. As they buckled their selves into the seats, her mother took her hand and held it tight for a moment. Azalea knew her mother was trying to be comforting, reassuring, but her stomach started to turn again. She dreaded the possibilities of what she could find when they finally arrived.

The cab drudged slowly down the packed streets. Looking at the time on her phone, she could see why. 5PM. Rush hour everywhere. People rushing to get home to their loved ones. The streets were crammed with car after car, loud engines halted as their owners honked angrily at people who also remained stuck in the stream out of the hectic centre. Knowing that they were going to be stuck for a while, Azalea decided to try Tabby again. Maybe she would pick up. Maybe she'd be okay and they could all enjoy an evening on the town as they laughed and joked about Azalea's crazy paranoia, dragging her far from her comfort zone to check that one person was okay.

"Welcome to the voicemail…" Azalea hangs up. There's no point leaving yet another message when Tabby hadn't responded to the last thousand.

"It'll be okay," her mother soothed, wrapping her arm around her. "She's probably just broken her phone or charger." She stroked the top of Azalea's head, her fingers tangling with the knots which she fought every morning.

She let her mother keep stroking her hair until they pulled outside. She felt calm to the core until the hand was retracted and her bubble of sanctuary burst. Opening the door, she was greeted by a cool breeze that crept under her layers and against her bare spine. The driver murmured a price as her mother placed the money in his hands.

"Keep the change," she urged desperation creeping in her voice. It was clear she didn't want to be far from Azalea's side, not right now, not when the world could come crashing down at any moment. She reached her side and looked at her apprehensively and Azalea knew her mother was debating whether or not she should let her go inside. She could see the coin toss going on behind her mother's eyes. Tails, she lets Azalea go up. Heads, she hails that taxi before it leaves and they go back to the station, head back home, head back to the safe little village and away from the scary, dangerous city, filled with drugs and drink and danger.

She stared intently at her mother, waiting for the okay to start heading upstairs, and her mother knew it. The coin must have landed in her favour as her mother nodded. Leading the way, Azalea noted how the out of order sign still hung, dusty as ever, over the lift doors. She let out an inpatient huff. How she loathed the stairs with a passion.

Flight by flight, she grimaced as every emotion built up inside her, trying to surface but being constantly drowned by another. There was so much going on in her head, she felt like she was being crushed from the inside. With every step, her thoughts became darker, twisting every little thing until all she saw was greys and blacks. Her heart was racing like the ticking clock on a bomb. She knew she was going to explode. No calming method in the world could make her lungs feel lighter and her breathing become rational.

Finally, they made it up all 13 floors. Azalea could barely stand, taking a moment to lean against the wall to catch her breath yet no matter how deep the breaths she still couldn't feel any relief. She waited for her mother to take her hand and then she walked the few steps to flat 13B.

Her knuckles rapped against the wooden door. They waited a second. Five. Thirty. A minute. No response. She knocked again, and again, every knock getting louder and louder until her knuckles were aching and reddened. She sat down across from the door as her mother took over the knocking.

She had to be here, she thought to herself, where else could she be? Her mind was blank. There were only three places her mind could put Tabby. Her bedroom, the campsite and here. She had to be here, Azalea argued with her inner self, there's nowhere else she could be. Standing up and dragging herself back to the door, she started hitting hard.

"Come on, Tabs!" She yelled at the shut door, hitting it hard and kicking it for added impact. The door shook on its' hinges but there was still no answer.

"Is there anywhere else she could be?" Her mother asked in her motherly tone, trying to soothe with the calm, friendly notes of her voice. Azalea shook her head. No, she knew Tabby was here. It was the only place she could be. She kept hitting and kicking whilst the door shook and creaked until an idea popped into her head. If she wasn't coming out, she'd go in.

She took a few steps away before slamming her entire body weight into the wooden panels. Again and again she threw her body hard against it as her mother urged her to stop.

"Azalea, please!" Her mother shouted, trying to be louder than the chaos that she was causing, "Please just stop. She's not here. Let's just go to a hotel and try again tomorrow or something." It was hard to ignore the pleading tone in her mother's voice, but Azalea knew she had to. Again, again, again, she slammed into the door. She was going to keep going until either she was too sore or until the door finally gave in. Finally, as if it swung open on its' own accord, the door gave way and Azalea's full force went tumbling into Tabby's flat.

Bursting into the flat, nearly toppling head over heels, the smell hit her like a brick. It was like nothing she'd ever smelt before and something she would never wish to smell again. She didn't even need to step further to know what that smell was. The tears started to escape before she could even control them, and she didn't know if it was her emotions causing it or the odour.

Death was the only friend

I'd known

She's walked behind me

Always clung close to my shadow

Like a child clinging to its' favourite toy

Waiting

Whispering

Promising

As the whispers grew to shouts

And the waiting became inpatient

And the promises became persistent

And the years grew hard

And the tears grew sharp

And the heart grew brittle

I finally knew

It was time to go see

My old friend

So I took the first

And my last step

Knowing that it would all be okay

As the F train came racing on

Chapter 20

The smell that confronted her turned her stomach inside out. She found it near impossible not to empty the contents of her stomach there and then, all over Tabby's floor. What was Tabby's floor. Before she even moved towards the room, she felt for her phone. Typing the three digits in and held the phone to her ear.

"Hello? I need..." she hesitated before sighed hard, "I don't know. Whoever you call out for a corpse." The operator kept talking, but Azalea didn't know what to say. She handed the phone to her mother, unable to speak any further. She watched as her mother walked around the hallway, holding her breath as much as possible, answering whatever questions the operator was asking. Azalea tried to focus on the words being spoken, but her head just wouldn't let her. There was too much going on up there.

In her wildest dreams, she'd never imagined that Tabby would be dead. Any thought like that was supposed to just be her paranoia talking, her anxiety preying on the slightest insecurity, her nightmares running away with themselves. She was supposed to be sat here, waiting, surprised. Happy that Azalea had come all this way for nothing, just because she was worried. They were supposed to order a takeaway and enjoy this evening, her mum having gone back to the hotel room so they could have alone time. Watch some films and gossip. Get up-to-date on each other's lives. Tabby was supposed to apologise for all the worry she caused and explain exactly what happened last time they were together. She was supposed to be honest and let Azalea in. She was supposed to share all her deep dark secrets and listen to Azalea's in return. She was supposed to still be full of life, weird and wonderful. She was supposed to be a lot of things, but none of them were dead.

Azalea couldn't help it. The tears had started to flood her eyes. Her body felt too heavy, the earth beckoning her to sink into it. She leaned against a wall, trying to stop herself from slipping to the ground. In that moment, she wasn't only grieving for Tabby. She was grieving for the moments that were, the moments that could have been and the moments that never will be. They had so many plans and now they were all gone, turned to dust and blown away by the breeze. She couldn't hold back and the buckets that built up in her tear ducts dripped until they steadily flew in a stream. She just watched as her mother continued to pass the room, lips moving fast.

Once the call was over, her mother took her hand and squeezed. "Come on," her mother urged, pulling her away from the wall she had collapsed into and towards the front door. Her body reluctantly followed, no longer sure how to react. All she could do was cry. Her chest felt as if she was being crushed from the inside. Her heart, which had been slowly healing, was torn to shreds. With every step she took, another thought emerged, pushing her deeper into the darkness her mind was forming and building around her like a fort. The thoughts of self-harm, suicide and pain played on repeat, no matter how much she fought against them. She barely survived Poppy, when she felt somewhat normal. Somewhat okay. How was she meant to cope when the source of her happiness was taken away from her, ripped away as fast as a plaster, leaving her red raw and sore to touch.

Her mother still hadn't let go of her hand and she hated it. She didn't want to be touched right now. She didn't want to be comforted. She wanted to be left to her woe and sorrow, her own specialised pity party catering specifically to the grief she felt only she knew. She glared at her mother as she squeezed her hand once more. As if she felt the hatred being directed her way, her mother looked her in the eyes and gave her a light smile before finally letting go. Azalea took her hand into her own and looked at the floor, sinking down the wall until she was finally sat on the cold, hard wooden floor.

She and her mother waited in the hallway, keeping the door as closed as possible to stop the smell from escaping further. Even the smell of damp that lurked in the walls smelt better than the decaying girl who lay a few rooms over, separated merely by a few walls. It felt like hours until the police finally met her on the 13th floor outside Tabby's flat with the coroner in tow.

As the officers and coroner made their way into the flat, Azalea held her breath. Even though she knew Tabby was long gone from the world of the living, part of her, a miniscule part, clung to the hope that the coroner would find a pulse. All those wishes were dashed when a few moments later, the coroner returned with the help of an officer, carrying a body bag out of the door and started to descend the stairs.

"Azalea?" Another officer questioned. He was a tall gentleman with silver hair and golden eyes. In any other circumstances, she and her mother would have probably called him a stud but not today. He kept glancing between her and her mother. "Felicity?" Her mother nodded lightly, her eyes also focusing on Azalea. She felt her cheeks start to instinctively flush red from the attention and found herself staring at their shoes.

"If you'd just like to follow us to the station, ladies. We have a few questions we need to ask. All standard procedure, don't worry." The officer smiled, his impeccable teeth glistening. As her mother agreed and started to trail after the officer down the many flights of stairs, Azalea took a deep breath.

Sat in the corridor, fluorescent lights blinding their retinas from above, Azalea waited for her mother to return to her side. She'd been taken in to explain the situation to the officers as to why they were found in a flat with a corpse. Of course, Tabby's death had already been ruled a death by overdose. It took the police five seconds to figure that one out when they searched her name and found she had previous, similar episodes in various A&Es in the city. Usually though, she'd have her stomach pumped instead of being stored on an ice-cold metal slab until her family claimed her.

Her mother finally came back with two cups of strong black coffee, one in each hand. Offering Azalea the cup, she took it with mumbled thanks.

"Sweetie," her mother sighed, "The officers just want a little chat with you before we get going home." She placed a hand on Azalea's head and slowly stroked it, the way Azalea had seen her mother calm the cats prior to the annual vet check-up many times before. She looked away, focusing intently on the police station's one water fountain a few feet away from where they sat.

"Have you not told them everything we know?" Azalea asked seriously, fighting the flight instinct building in her gut.

"I have, darling, but they want to hear from you. It's just procedure, a few questions and we will be on our way."

She knew that even if she persuaded her mother she couldn't, that wouldn't matter to the police. She stood up and raised the cup to her lips before taking a long sip. It'd be easier to do it all now whilst it's still fresh, her mind urged her. She couldn't argue anymore. "Let's get this over with." She murmured in her mother's direction as she headed in the direction of the officer waiting patiently for her.

She followed the officer to a room that looked eerily like an interrogation room from a police film. She wondered, as she looked at the male and female officer already sat at the table, who was the good cop and who was the bad copy. She sat in the chair furthest from the door, her mother sitting at her side.

"Hello, Azalea," the female officer's voice was soft and warm as she spoke to her, "Your mother has explained what you were doing at the flat, but we'd like to hear it in your own words if that's fine?" Azalea nodded lightly, not sure if any words would ever be able to find her again.

Pressing at something in front of him, it was at that moment that Azalea noted the male officer had a tablet lay before him on the table. With a few more taps, a recording app was started and a red blinking text flashed the words 'recording in process' on the screen.

"Firstly, Azalea, can you just confirm your full name for us and your age," the female officer proceeded.

Biting her bottom lip, Azalea fidgeted, struggling to get comfortable in the chair. She knew it wasn't the seat making her uncomfortable. She forced herself to speak, willing it to be over and done with as soon as possible.

"My name is Azalea Rose Hart, and I'm 17."

"And why, Miss Hart, were you at the residence of Tabitha Dixon tonight?" A faint smile hung on the female officer's lips, urging her further.

"I hadn't heard from Tabby, Tabitha, for a few weeks and the last time I was here, she didn't seem right. You know. Mentally," Azalea looked at the table between them, hoping the world would swallow her whole. "She had an episode and sent me home. We didn't speak for a while, but when she got back in contact it went back to the normal amount of contact before she disappeared off the map again. I got worried." She felt her left hand clench tightly. "I just wish I'd come sooner. I might have been able to stop her."

"What do you mean by an episode, Azalea?" the male officer queried, an unreadable expression on his face.

"Well, we met at a counselling retreat for mentally unstable teens." Azalea bit her bottom lip, hoping he didn't comment on her attitude in his report. She already felt bad, she didn't need him labelling her as uncooperative in the interview process as well. "She had depressive episodes and it seemed like she was on one of those, but there was just more to it. She didn't want to talk about it and when I pressed, she kicked me out."

"And the last time you spoke, did she seem depressed to you?"

Azalea looked guiltily at the table. She didn't know. The last time they spoke, everything seemed fine. Tabby was her usual self. The same sarcastic, melodramatic, sweet, caring girl that she was when they met. Had Tabby been keeping her depression and the cause of it to herself? Did she not trust Azalea with her secrets after all?

"I don't know.." She could feel her voice breaking alongside the rest of her and it seemed like the police officers knew it too. Holding out a box of tissues to her, the female officer nodded.

"It's okay. I think that's all. It seems evident that Miss Dixon took her own life and we don't need to investigate into this further. I'd like to take your number if anything else arises, Mrs Hart, but I think that is all we need."

Her mother nodded and took the officers' hands as they are offered to her, one by one.

As they are getting ready to leave, a thought occurs to Azalea. "Wait, what about the body?" She asked.

"What do you mean?" The female officer asked, a confused look painting her relatively attractive face.

"Her body. Do you contact her family or whatever for funeral…" Before she could even finish her sentence, both officers were shaking their head.

The female officer spoke up. "Ms Dixon doesn't have any listed next of kin or relative from what we can see on both our database and the hospital's. Her body will be cremated by the council and buried in a communal plot if there is no one to collect it. Unfortunately, as you are not family or a next of kin, you can't claim her body otherwise we'd allow it to be passed to yourselves to make arrangements." The officers started heading out the room, patting Azalea's shoulders on their way. "Sorry, kid."

Finally excused from the station, Azalea left in a daze. It was only as she sat in that room answering the questions that she realised she was a terrible friend to Tabby. She clearly wasn't there when she needed her.

"Where to now?" Her mother asked, linking her arm tightly.

Azalea fought long and hard for a minute before answering. There was only one place she wanted to be right now.

"I want to say goodbye." She didn't even look at her mother. She knew her mother agreed, it was something that she needed to do to start the grieving process. Without that first goodbye, part of her might be waiting forever for Tabby to return.

She didn't know what magic her mother performed on the uniformed officer at the door, but she was allowed back into Tabby's flat for a few minutes. Unfortunately for him, her mother used to be a great squatter back in the day and could argue for hours about the rights not to move on. Azalea sat on the bed, listening in the distance to her mother explaining the situation to a new uniformed officer as what was originally just a quick visit to say goodbye became a 22 minute sit-in and counting. The police officer was trying to urge them along repeatedly and the words were becoming harder by the minute. Azalea couldn't move yet though. Now that Tabby's body had gone, she found she had no energy left inside of her. She felt like jelly, inside and out. She just continued to stare at the phoenix through the doorway, looking over the hallway as if she was guarding it from the bad thoughts of the past. Was the rainbow phoenix the last thing

Tabby saw, she wondered. She rearranged herself slightly on the bedspread to see if there was a better angle when she heard a crinkle of something under the blanket she was sat on.

Lifting the blanket back, Azalea found a crumbled sheet of paper, somewhat crunched with writing on one side. Her eyes were so sore from all the tears she'd cried and how much she'd rubbed, it took them a moment for them to adjust enough to register what she held in her hand. She skimmed the writing quickly, picking out her own name. She read it again repeatedly, until the words were branded in her mind. She called loudly for help, unable to move any of her extremities. In her hand, she held Tabby's last words to the world. She remained still as an officer appeared and took the note from her. He slunk away as quietly as he came in and she was grateful because she knew, in that moment, she wouldn't be able to do anything but cry.

To whomsoever it may concern,

I never knew I could be this formal in death, but I don't know who will find me or this note, or if anyone will before I am so badly decomposed that I no longer resemble a human being.

If you are the authorities of any kind, this was a suicide. Not a well-planned one, but the best ones never are.

To my foes, sorry but I beat you to the punchline. You can't hurt me once I'm dead. Sorry Olly, I can only die once, as much as I know you wanted to do it.

To my friends, I'm sorry. I love you, but it got too much. I couldn't keep putting on a smiling face and pretending to be okay. We all knew I wasn't okay, but I kept smiling and laughing like I didn't care. I did. Too much. He marked me and I knew no matter how I tried 'Victim' would always be the first thing any of you saw when you thought of me. And I'm no victim, I won't let myself be called that. Not even now I'm dead.

Az, Grandpa (not like you'd even remember reading this, or that you'd ever be here to find it so I guess to whichever of his carers has to read my pathetic suicide note to him), I couldn't help myself and I didn't want to be a burden. Neither of you deserve my being making your life worse and now I have taken that option from you anyway. You don't need to worry about me now. I'm sure hell is warm this time of year. I will never forget everything you have done for me. I love you.

Always yours, Tabby

Chapter 21

Holding the note in her hand, Azalea couldn't help but cry. She thought she had run dry, but it was clearly not the case. Tabby's cursive curls just cut deeper into her heart. She cursed at herself more and more every time she pictured the words. How did she not see that Tabby needed help? How did no one see? Reading that note made it blatantly obvious that something was wrong. How was it possible that no one knew? How was it possible she didn't know? She thought she'd known Tabby well, but it was undeniable. She'd never known her at all.

She could feel the anger rising up from the pit of her stomach, singeing everything in its' wake. All she wanted to do was punch something. Hard. Until her fists bled and her wrists were broken. Until she stopped seeing a red blur covering her vision. Until the pain in her chest stopped. Until her heart stopped breaking and cracking and shattering. She never thought she'd feel a pain like this again. In that instant, a thought clicked in her mind. She wasn't the only one who'd feel this pain, she was just the first to know. She had to let the others know, so she wasn't alone in the world. So she wasn't the only one grieving a girl that could have been saved.

Fumbling, she ran her hand along the top of the blanket. It had to be here somewhere. She'd never known a fellow teenager with the willpower to not have their phone within a 2 feet radius.

Finally, she hit jackpot. The phone had run out of juice, but that was fine. Pocketing it and its charger, she headed to the door. Her mother apologised once more to the officer then they were on their way back to the hotel.

As they walked, Azalea told her mother the plan. She shook her head profusely. "Azalea Rose Hart, you are the only person I know of who is dumb enough to steal from a crime scene."

"It's not a crime scene," Azalea argued, "The only reason an officer was still there was so no one stole whilst they were waiting for the lock to be fixed." Catching her mother's glare out of the corner of her eye, she continued. "Anyway, someone needs to let Azalea's grandfather know. The police don't even know he exists!"

"Exactly!" Her mother countered, "You should have left it to the police to do. They would have sorted it out if you'd given them the phone when you found it!"

"Mum, it would be so impersonal if the police did it. They don't know Tabby! They don't know how amazing she…" the words caught in her throat as she realised she was still using present tense. Tabby was gone. She wasn't going to come back.

Her mother took her hand and squeezed it tight, walking a few stops ahead to stop Azalea in her tracks. "Darling, that's why it's better if the police did it. You are too close to this. You were Tabby's friend. It's going to hit you hard every time you talk about her. It hit me every time I talked about Poppy with my counselling group and it took a while…"

Azalea stopped her mother. "You went to counselling? When? I never knew."

Her mother rolled her eyes and scoffed before responding. "Oh yeah, why wouldn't I tell my grieving child that I couldn't handle my own grief? I didn't want you to bear that on your shoulders." Spotting a bench a little further on, her mother dragged her over and they both took a seat. "The grief hit me bad and I thought if you knew I wasn't taking it well that would stop you trying to process." She wrapped her arm around Azalea's shoulder and squeezed her tightly, bringing her in as close as she could. "And then you tried to kill yourself and I knew that we both had to do something about it. We couldn't live in our grief like that, it was killing us and I wasn't ready to lose both of my daughters. One was enough."

Azalea took in her mother's face for a moment. Tired, aging with tears forming as she scrunched her face in to fight their release. She lowered herself, resting her head on her mother's shoulder. She wrapped her loose arm around her mother's waist. She felt her mother's body relax as she clung closer. Her mother's hand reached over and played with her hair, stroking it in the soothing manner she always used to do when she was an upset little girl.

"I know, mum, I know. I just…" Azalea let out a deep sigh, "I don't want some officer to break this old man's heart and then go on like they'd never done it."

"I know, my love," her mother cooed as she continued running her fingers through the loose strands, "And that's why I'm not going to stop you. If you think it's what's best, you can be the one to call. Just don't let it put you back in that box you went into after Poppy, okay?"

Azalea nodded, not sure what to say. As she lay there, her mother slowly soothing her, she wish her mother could know just how grateful she was for everything, but she didn't know what quite to say.

"I love you, mum," those words were all she could fathom in that moment. Her own tears had finally caught up with her as she lay thinking about Tabby and Poppy and everything that had ever happened in her lifetime.

Her mother lightly smiled as a few of her tears escaped. "I love you too, Az."

Azalea hesitated, flicking her eyes between the screens. It didn't take long to find Tabby's grandfather's carer on her phone, but the nerves had started eating at her. She glanced, for the umpteenth time, checking that she got every digit right before finally hitting the call button on her mobile.

"Hello?" The voice on the other end of the phone asked.

"Hi, is this Bernie?" Azalea asked, hopeful. She'd hate for this number that was so important in finding Tabby's grandfather to be outdated and used by someone else.

"Hi, yes. What's this about?" The woman sounded impatient but Azalea understood why. It was getting towards 6PM, the usual hour cold callers bombarded anyone with a number they could get their hands on. Always in time to interrupt teatimes as they knew people were likely to be getting home from their 9 to 5 jobs.

"Hi, Bernie. This is Azalea. I'm a friend of Tabby's. She's why I'm calling actually."

As soon as she heard Tabby's name, Bernie's voice changed. More delicate, less robotic and agitated. More caring. "Oh god, what's wrong? Is she okay?" She could hear the panic in Bernie's voice as she heard the other woman scrambling on the other end. She could almost hear the gears turning in Bernie's head through the phone. "I hadn't heard from her for a while, but that's just Tabby for you, she could be distant."

"She…" Azalea sucked in what felt like all the air in the room and willed herself to continue. "I found her dead this morning, Bernie. She…" she hesitated, not sure how to word it. "She…"

She heard a whimper from Bernie. "It - It's okay, I-I get what you're trying to say," the voice stammered between weeps. "The police?"

Azalea fought the urge to nod along, scared her voice would break. "They know. I called them as soon as... as soon as I found her."

"How?"

"Pills, they said. That's what they found anyway. I got your number from her phone. You know, so someone could let her grandfather know. He wasn't listed as a next of kin or relative..."

Bernie stopped her before she could go on, "No, he wouldn't be, dear. He's in a care home and has been for a long while. Tab never had anyone listed after he went in. She had no other family."

"But..." She felt the words slipping from her tongue and vaporizing in the air. Tabby was practically alone in the world. She shouldn't have let Tabby ever leave her sight.

"Don't worry, dear," Bernie continued, "I'll call the police and I'll let them know that she has a next of kin, not that it really matters.

I imagine they have already started processing the body and they'll be annoyed I'm complicating their paperwork." She exhaled hard, light tears still echoing in her voice. "I'll take care of it all."

"What about her grandad?" Azalea asked urgently, "Will you tell him?"

Bernie was hesitant on the other end of the call. "He's got dementia, dear, he barely remembered Tabby. It's probably not in his best interest."

"Best interest!" Azalea exclaimed, "She was his granddaughter! Yes, knowing she's dead is probably in his best interest!"

"Yes, dear, I know," Bernie urged patiently, "I know but it might affect him more mentally than you think. It would be best to ask the home what they advise…"

Azalea could feel the anger welling up in her again. "What the home advise?!" She felt the sudden urge to throw her phone against the wall. "Fuck. That. He needs to know. She wanted him to know. She said. In her note." With every word, her eyes were welling up, frustrating her more. She wished she'd let her mother sit in the room for this instead of urging her to the bar for some privacy, letting her know she'd be fine on her own. All she wanted right now was her mother's arms around her, professing that it was all going to be okay.

"Fine," Bernie said bluntly. "If you want him to know that his only living relative killed herself, you tell him! I'll send you the details." She thought she heard Bernie mutter the words 'for fuck sake' and 'fucking bitch' but it was so low, she daren't ask her to repeat herself.

"Thank you!" Azalea felt relieved as she hung up the phone, taking a step closer to her goal. A few moments later, a text came through from Bernie. The care home wasn't close, but at least they could take a detour on the way home.

Her mother couldn't believe what she was saying when she arrived back at the hotel room, slightly tipsy. "What the actual fuck, Azalea?" She cursed.

"I couldn't let him not know," Azalea shook her head, refusing to believe she was doing something wrong.

"Then let the carer do it! Or the police!" Her mother facepalmed, sinking into the lone seat as Azalea paced. "Why Azalea?"

"He needs to know she was loved, mum. He needs to know…" The thoughts were faster than her lips. She wanted him to know that she was sorry. That she wished she could have saved her. That if she knew she would have done anything and everything to keep Tabby from taking all those pills. "He needs to know that he has actually lost her. He might not remember the conversation, but he needs to know that."

"But people with dementia sometimes struggle with that, sweetheart," her mother urged. "You don't have to do this. The home probably has a procedure for this. It can't be uncommon for a resident to lose a family member!"

"I don't care, mum," she cried, her voice breaking, "I need to do this. I do. Please?"

Her mother let out an exacerbated sigh of defeat. "Fine. But I'm coming with you. You're not doing this alone. We will go tomorrow." She stood and stumbled over to the double bed they were sharing for the night. "But if it goes wrong, you were warned." As her head hit the pillow, the snoring started to echo throughout the room. Walking over to the window, Azalea looked out to the city's skyline. She wished she could have shared how beautiful she found this world with Tabby, but it was too late.

It hadn't taken as long as they'd thought to get here by train, particularly as it seemed like the world was still asleep when they stumbled onto the platform. They'd arrived at the care home shortly after what was the residents' breakfast hour. Staring at the sign outside as they waited for the door to be opened, Azalea wasn't sure whether to be wary of nuns with a name like Saint Augustine's. She was imagining the black and white attire when a spectacled woman opened the door and ushered them into the reception area. After her mother painstakingly explained every molecular detail of the visit, it was agreed that they could see Tabby's grandfather.

"Mr Coles may not be completely there. Mentally I mean," the manager warned Azalea before she let them leave the office in pursuit of the nurse, "At this time of day, we can never really say how lucid the residents are. Sometimes they are having a great day and they remember everything, others they hit out in bursts of forgetful anger. Just be careful. Gerald has been known to hit out."

Azalea nodded as her mother took her hand, leading her out of the office and after the nurse down the corridor. The nurse showed them into an empty family room and left for a few minutes, returning with Tabby's grandfather in a wheelchair. Too nervous to sit, Tabby walked along the back wall, listening intensely to the nurse's instructions.

"Now," the nurse said as she sat Gerald across from her, "Mr Coles isn't very vocal nowadays but there may be moments when he sputters random nonsense or screams. Don't worry, this is usual. If you're worried at any point, just press this button," she pointed to the button located by the door with a small faded sticker of what should have been a nurse's cap. "It'll alert us in the nurse's station next door and we will be right through." The nurse left then, gliding through the door, it swinging back into place as if it'd never been disturbed in the first place. Her mother positioned herself at the back of the room, somewhat out of the way but still there if needed.

Standing across from him, she could tell he would have been a handsome young man back in the day. Now his hair was silver and scruffily tucked behind his ears whilst his eyes looked bleak and dead to his surroundings. She didn't know how she was going to tell him, or if he'd even understand what she was saying, but she knew it had to be done.

She could hear the reluctance in Bernie's voice echoing once more in her head when she mentioned telling him. Maybe she should have let Bernie deal with it. Let her call the police, let her and them figure out how to tell this old man the worst news he could probably think of, especially after losing his own child already. No, she thought, she'd feel guilty if she left it to someone else. She was the one who hadn't helped Tabby, she was the reason she was dead. She tried to push that thought back out of her head, but part of her clung to it. She knew it was true. She knew she wasn't there for Tabby like she should have been. Tabby wasn't a burden to her, no matter what the note said, she was a burden to Tabby. She should be the one who is dead.

"Mr Coles?" Azalea asked nervously, hoping for some kind of response.

Though he did not speak, he turned to look at her, a blatant sadness in his eyes. Maybe, she thought, part of him already knew.

"Mr Coles," she continued, walking to the chair closest to him and sitting, her gaze intently focused on him. "I'm a friend of your granddaughter, Tabitha."

His eyes remained glued to her and she was disheartened when there was no sign of recognition from the name. Summoning her inner strength, she rummaged for her phone in her pocket. She knew she had a picture saved. Loading it up on her phone, she showed the elderly man the image. No words came, but his eyes lit up with a spark. She could tell he recognised her. His lips started to twitch and she braced herself for one of the screams she'd been warned about.

"Catherine?" He asked, his eyes focusing on the picture, his fragile fingers shakenly touching the screen.

"No," Azalea said shaking her head. "This is Catherine's daughter, Tabby."

As if the name clicked in part of his mind, a light smile creaked along his long face. "Tiny Tabby kitty cat," as she looked on, a tear rolled down his cheek. His eyes looked at her once more, as if looking into her, the sadness lingering.

She looked down at her hands and slowly interlocked and unlocked them repeatedly, not able to get comfortable. "She died, Mr Coles. I'm sorry."

The old man's face crumbled in on itself as he started to weep. She went to touch him lightly on the arm but he swung his arm violently at her, trying to hit her away. "No, no, no!" He screamed, swinging his arms wildly in all directions. Her mother was across the room in an instant, moving Azalea out of the way. Once she was clear of his arms, her mother ran to press the button. In an instant, two nurses and a security guard were in the room. The guard restrained his arms, holding them down by his sides, as the nurses went about calming him down. All Azalea could do was look as the old man repeatedly uttered the word 'no' as he was taken out of the room by one of the nurses and the guard.

The other nurse stood looking between Azalea and her mother. "I think it is best that you leave," she sternly said, pointing in the direction of the hallway. As they made it into the hallway, Azalea could see the devastated man being led into his room. She didn't know if he fully understood what she said but it was clear now just how fragile Tabby's grandfather was. She felt sick, knowing that she had urged everyone to let her talk to him. She had knowingly caused an elderly man she didn't know further mental harm. The nausea of the feeling became too overbearing and she found herself rushing outside to hunch over a patch of grass. A few dry heaves later, her mother helped her to her feet.

"Time to go home, kid," she said, stroking Azalea's back lightly. "You need to rest." With heavy feet and a heavy heart, Azalea let her mother lead her away from St Augustine's in the direction of the train station. All she wanted right now was to be alone, in bed, to sleep away the nightmare her life had become once more.

Chapter 22

Azalea climbed and climbed the multitude of stairs before her. The flights appeared to go on forever. She felt an ache throbbing up her legs. How long had she been climbing now? An hour? Three? She couldn't even fathom. Step by step, she climbed until it felt like the floor was burning into the soles of her feet. Only when the pain became excruciating did the stairs seem to finally stop on a landing. The thirteenth floor. As the door swung open on its own accord, a gust of foul air pushed Azalea through it. It slammed furiously, echoing through the corridor. The smell worsened as she walked slowly down the empty, dark space.

She urged her feet to stop walking as it dawned on her where she was going, but they continued to stumble down the corridor until they reached it. Flat 13B. Her feet landing on the carpet in front of the engraved slab, the door creaked inwards, exposing the hallway with its phoenix protector. The odour hit her even harder, nearly knocking her to the floor.

"Az," a voice called softly from the adjoining room. She knew it was quite impossible and wanted to flee, as fast as her little legs could take her, but they seemed to have a mind of their own. Striding, her legs took her further into the flat. The carpet crunched beneath her weight, as if it hadn't been touched in years. How long had it been since she was last here? She knew it couldn't have been more than a few weeks, but the flat looked nearly forgotten, with its masses of cobwebs and dust. Even the colour of the phoenix had begun to fade.

"Oh Azzy," another voice joined the call, a sweetness to its tone. She would recognise the voice as much as she recognised her own. Neither of these voices could be real. This had to be some sick twisted dream. Her thoughts were confirmed as her feet led her into the bedroom. On the edge of the bed sat Poppy, coated in a fresh layer of blood and dirt, as if she'd pulled herself out of her own grave just to wait for her sister.

"Hello, sissy," her sister cooed, "come to see Tabby so soon?"

"Poppy?" She asked, so unsure of what she was seeing. This was definitely a dream. There was no possible way this could happen. She tried to peer around her sister at Tabby, but with every movement, Poppy blocked her view.

"I'm not sure you're ready for this," her sister said knowingly. "Your heart isn't ready for it."

Azalea shook her head. "Please Poppy," she begged "I'm ready."

"If you insist." Poppy shrugged as one of her arms fell loose, landing on the floor as more blood pulsated from her chest wounds. Poppy rose to her feet and walked to Azalea's side. "But I did warn you." Before her eyes, Poppy disappeared. Azalea's eyes were drawn to Tabby, hoping to see a living version of her. Her stomach turned as her eyes glanced upon the rotting corpse of her once best friend. Flies and maggots crawled through all the bite marks they'd caused in the skin, exposing muscle and bone to the world. The smell of death intensified as she watched the insects wriggle and squirm. As she stared, she saw the eyes blink to life. Hesitantly she moved closer, preparing to speak. Forming the words, she noticed the left eye begin to twitch. Within a moment, a worm burst through the socket, pushing a half-nibbled eyeball out of its way. The words no longer there, a scream leapt out of Azalea's lips.

With a sudden jolt, Azalea was awake. Thank god, she let out a sigh of relief as she tried to calm her heart rate with deep breaths as it thumped too hard against her ribcage. Just a nightmare. She was safe from the overwhelming presence of death and its aftermath. Weeks had passed since Azalea stumbled into that bleak room with the foul odour she could still feel up her nostrils. She stared at her phone for a moment, her eyes adjusting to the brightness. 5:43AM. She begrudgingly made her way out of her bed and went about the same routine she'd had since she and her mother had gotten back: a quick bathroom trip with a detour to the kitchen for snacks and drinks before heading back to bed. She had decided that it was time to let the depression win. She'd attended college for all of a day that week, it just felt too much to handle. She'd lost too much for her life to be normal anymore. Losing Poppy had been heart-breaking, but losing a new friend whilst still grieving the biggest death in her life at that point? Her soul had been crushed to a million itty bitty pieces and would never be whole again. She'd happily never exist if it meant she could escape the constant aching of reality without two of the strongest women she knew. She could never be as strong as they were, no matter how hard she tried. Getting back into her bed, she pulled her quilt over her head, trying to send psychic messages to the cats hoping they'd appear for soothing cuddles. She knew there'd be no chance of that though, given the unnaturally clear skies that had yet to break above her. They'd be out all day and night if they didn't have to return to eat occasionally, with Storm usually trailing giddily behind Dali, their hunt between her teeth.

Azalea had hoped that after Bernie had contacted the police about Tabby having a next of kin, she could at least have some form of official goodbye. A funeral for all the people who'd loved her and cared for her. It never happened. It was all done swiftly with no major attention drawn to the tragic demise of a young woman. She'd received a call back from Bernie afterwards explaining that due to Tabby's grandfather's mental impairment, it wouldn't be fair to have a funeral. A cremation had been arranged and the ashes had been buried in silence alongside Tabby's parents in the family plot with no one except the cemetery's custodian present.

She must have dozed back off as the next thing she knew, she was being blinded by the sun. She hadn't even noticed the quilt being moved from over her head. Blinking, she could see the blur of her mother moving closer to the bed whilst another blur curled by her toes. Her mother had already perched herself on the end by the time Azalea's eye had focused.

"Az, it's time to get up and out," her mother pleadingly ordered, a harsh undertone lingering in her voice, "You can't stay in bed forever." She lightly stroked Storm's chin, her focus taken away from Azalea as the cat purred beneath her fingers.

"I can try," Azalea murmured, trying to pull the sheets back over her.

"No chance!" Her mother shouted, grabbing the quilt and yanking it to the floor. "You need to get up, Az. Now."

She sat up, anger bubbling in her stomach. "Mum! I am grieving. Leave me alone! It's not like I want to feel this way!" The urge to break things rising, she threw her phone across the room, barely missing her mother.

"Azalea Rose Hart, you will chill the fuck out!" Her mother roared, her fists clenched. "You will get the fuck out of your bed now, and we are taking you to the doctor's! You need help, girl, and I swear you are fucking going to get it!" In an instant, her mother grabbed her wrist and ripped her out of bed and nearly out of her room.

"I-I…" Azalea found herself stammering. "P-Please mum, no. I-I-I can't. I can't." She felt herself crumbling in on herself as her weight became too much for her legs to hold.

Her mother dropped to her side and cradled her tightly. "I know, baby, I know." Stroking her cheek, she wiped away any loose tears. "You need to though. Neither of them would want this. You'd only just started to become yourself again, don't do this. Not now. You were doing so well."

Listening to her mother, Azalea could hear the sadness that still ambled through her mother's voice. She knew she was being selfish. She wasn't the only one grieving, but the deaths ate at Azalea so frivolously, devouring every thought of anguish and despair like an all-you-can-eat buffet. She knew she wasn't but part of her head was still trying to convince her she was to blame for it all and at the moment it was winning. For Poppy. For

Tabby. She was the one who hadn't noticed. She was the one who wasn't there. She could have stopped Hunter from murdering her sister in the kitchen below her room. If only she'd stayed in that night. She could have been with Tabby, stopped her from even getting to a point where death seemed like the only feasible option. She knew she could never change the past, but she clung to the lingering thoughts of how all of it could have been different. If only she'd been more attentive. If only she'd been less self-centred and more present. If only she'd noticed the warning signs. If only she'd picked up on the situations at hand. She could have saved them both.

"I know you're blaming yourself," her mother continued, her hand now stroking her hair. "But you couldn't have stopped either. You're not a clairvoyant, Az, you didn't know what was going to happen and no one would have expected you to." Her mother lowered her head onto Azalea's and squeezed her as tight as was possible. Azalea sat there weeping in her mother's arms, wishing the pain would stop.

"I think it's time for you to go back to counselling, my love," her mother suggested, an authoritative tone mixed amongst caring words.

"I-I-I…" Azalea wanted to argue, but she knew her mother's words were true and no matter what it took, her mother was going to drag her back to sessions. She decided to change her approach. "With Poppy…" She hesitated, not sure how to ask or if it would still be distressing for her mother. She didn't want to hurt her anymore. "Was it…"

"Hard? Difficult? Similar to where you attended? Absolutely bullshit?" Azalea nodded along, just wanting an answer to anything really. Something reassuring.

"At first, it nearly was the death of me," her mother went on, "But I knew I needed it. I knew that I couldn't let the depression take me down. With how bad it was, they advised me to go to the doctor's too. They started me on some medication and it helped and has been helping. It had some bad effects but it was worth it in the end. I'm still here, and I'm better than I was. Partly thanks to the medication, partly to the counselling, but mostly because of you. I knew I could never leave you alone. You needed me, so I needed to be me and stick around."

"What if I need meds? I don't want to be on drugs for this." Azalea cried, unsettled by the thought.

"They're a good helping hand if they're needed," her mother hushed her, lightly kissing her on the top of the head. "You might need them, you might not. But if you do, there's nothing wrong with it. It's not permanent. Just until you're feeling better."

Azalea thought long and hard for a moment. She knew she couldn't keep going along how she was and any help was better than nothing. "Can we," she asked quietly, "can we go to the doctor's tomorrow?"

"Of course, sweetheart," her mother soothed as Azalea rested her weight into her mother. They sat there for a while in silence, just curled into each other on the bedroom floor, as the cats paraded around them, eager for some attention.

After a long conversation with her doctor and mother, it was decided that Azalea might feel better with a light dose of something to help with the depression. It felt weird to her, openly discussing her mental health. Even after her suicide attempt, it wasn't discussed much after she left the hospital. She'd been asked if she was okay once by her GP and that was that. No follow-up, no intervention. Maybe she should have been more open then, she thought, instead of shrugging and saying she was doing okay.

"You might not feel great at first, Azalea, but that's okay. It can take a few weeks for it to properly start to kick in," the doctor explained, "but if you still feel like this after a month or so, or if you feel worse, we can always change it to another type for you that might be better suited."

Her mother nodded. "Yeah, Az, at first you might feel worse but I'll be there all the way through it. No matter what, I'm not going anywhere."

"And if needed, you can always come back to talk or ask anything. Just tell the receptionist when you call up I've said you can be seen whenever it's needed and I'll make sure I let the staff know."

"Thank you, doctor," her mother said as she took the prescription from the doctor's hand.

"Thanks," Azalea murmured as she rose to her feet and followed her mother out of the room. Medication and counselling, the doctor had said, would probably be her best bet to feeling somewhat better. She wandered slowly behind her mother as she made her way to the pharmacy down the street. She'd decided she'd listen to the doctor this time. If the pills didn't work, there wasn't much to be done. She just hoped her first counselling session, booked for the afternoon as an urgent appointment thanks to her mother's pleading, went well. She was ready to get her problems out in the open. She needed to vent everything somehow, even if it meant sharing it all with a person she didn't know. In a hazed blur, Azalea continued to follow her mother for the rest of the day as her mind ran away with itself.

The next thing Azalea knew, her appointment time had arrived and she was sat across from a woman with straight blonde hair and lake blue eyes. Her pink lips were formed into a light caring smile. Azalea couldn't help but survey her appearance and take her all in. From the top of her head, to the bottom of her slightly heels shoes, the woman was prim and proper. Not a strand of hair out of place. Almost as perfect and neat as a doll, without all the unrealistic shapes. Azalea had never met anyone who looked this feminine yet strong at the same time. Everything about this woman was urging her to spill her guts, to confess all her deep dark secrets at a moment's notice. There was something about her that just vibed as trustworthy.

"Hi," the woman smiled calmly, "I'm Lily White. You're Azalea, right?" Lily's kindness was shining through in her words. All the anxiety Azalea had felt at first had melted away.

"Right," Azalea nodded, getting ready to settle in for the session ahead.

"For this first session, I think it would be best to just get the outline down as to why you're here. You can keep it as brief as you want and if you think I'm pushing or if I ask too many questions: just tell me to shut up, okay?" Lily's smile became larger, turning into a glistening grin.

Azalea couldn't help it, her own grin forming. She felt completely comfortable here. Maybe her mother and the doctor were right. Maybe this time around, the counselling will help. "Okay," she replied, finding herself surprisingly calm.

"Ready?" Lily asked, a pen in hand already with its nib pressed against the paper, waiting to start scribbling down whatever words spluttered out of her mouth.

"Ready." Azalea nodded, taking in a deep breath and preparing for the words to tumble into the world, not overthinking what to say for once or if her own words would make her appear crazy. She closed her eyes and let the words flow free, without a care in the world.

Chapter 23

She fell into a routine easily. A pill in the morning every day before college. A call twice a week with Lily, plus an evening session every Wednesday. Swimming on Saturdays, a recommended physical exercise she actually seemed to enjoy. She was trying hard this time. She was determined to get better, no matter what it took. After a few weeks on the medication, she started to feel more like her old self. She took baby steps into becoming more social. She was trying to make friends. But today, she didn't want to do anything but mope.

She knew it would hit her hard today of all days, but she never knew it would be this bad. She was in a permanent state of anxiousness and just wanted to live hidden away from the world for the rest of her days. Aside from a "birthday breakfast" consisting of bacon, sausage, hash browns and pancakes, there was no reason for Azalea to be happy. It was just a day she had no one to spend it with. Her mother tried to get her out of the funk but after half an hour, she gave up and headed for work. There was no encouragement to go to college at least. She knew being around people practically strangers would just make her worse.

She had discussed it with Lily earlier in the week, how grief could affect life events meant to be positive. She'd only started properly adjusting to post-Poppy life but her birthday pushed her back. She missed the knock on her door at 3:27am, the time she was born, with her birthday cupcake sparkling with its perched candle. Poppy's sing-song voice wishing her the greatest birthday in the world. Sitting up for hours until they fell asleep, Azalea in Poppy's arms. It was weird, only waking up because her body wanted her to, not because someone was tickling her feet or whispering her name down her ear, the hot air making her flick it away. It may have been Azalea's birthday, but Poppy was always the one who made it feel like it. Without her, it just felt like a typical Thursday.

It was around midday when she finally rolled out of bed and only due to Dali scratching at her toes. She knew if she didn't feed him soon, he'd happily eat her toes. She stumbled down the stairs, head still too tired to properly function, two cats attempting to trip her down the steps. Her furry feet guards directed her towards their food bowls in the kitchen, purring along the way. Throwing some wet food in their dishes, she was abandoned immediately. Of course, food will always be number one in her fur babies' eyes.

Maybe, she thought, if she focused on her college work today she could forget what date it was completely. Moving around the cats and counter, she flicked on the kettle. She needed some caffeine if she was going to get through the day. She wasn't a particular fan of tea but she knew if she dumped enough milk and sugar in it, she'd be able to dip her biscuits in it without the risk of burning the roof of her mouth. She glanced at the clock, perched high on the wall. 1:23PM. Just another 11 hours until today was over.

Unfortunately, the day seemed to drag for a week. She tried to do everything she could think of to take her mind off being alone. Reading. College work. Playing with the cats. She hoped by the next time she looked towards the clock, it would be around 6PM at least, nearer to her mother's home time, but when she swept her eyes over the time it was barely 3PM.

With nothing else to do, her mind kept wandering to thoughts of Tabby. She knew she had to move forward with her own life, but it still felt too soon. She hadn't known Tabby as well as she'd thought, but she was still a big part of her life even if she'd only been around for a blip in her timeline. She came smashing in like a wrecking ball, knocking down all the rubble and making way for something new. Part of Azalea had loved her, possibly as even more than a friend. Their time together had been too short. Outside of video calls and texts, they'd seen each other for a total of 2 weeks, but it felt like she'd known Tabby all of her life.

Maybe, she thought, if she'd known everything could have been different. She could have saved Tabby from herself. Maybe, with time, they could have fallen in love with each other and that would be that. No need to worry about the toxic men who'd passed through their lives because the other would always be there. Azalea tried to push the thoughts out of her mind. She couldn't think about what the future could have been. It was all just a fantasy now. The future would never be what she thought it would be, but that was okay. It had to be okay. There was nothing she could do about it, either way. All she could do was live it.

Taking her cup of tea and a packet of chocolate digestives, she made her way back upstairs to bed. It would take a long time to move on, but she knew she had to do it. She had no other option. No other way out. Sitting on her desk chair, she lifted the lid of her laptop, the screen flicking to life. A cheeky smile gleamed back at her. She stroked the screen, wishing she could feel Tabby's cheek behind her fingertips but she knew, eventually, she'd start to feel more like herself again. The medication seemed to be helping, to some extent at least.

She didn't even notice her mother had returned home, she was too focused looking through all the photos on her laptops. Pictures of Poppy, their mother. So many family moments that she'd love to live again. Even just photos from last year felt so long ago. Had it really been that long, she thought, since she last felt like she had a family?

"That's a nice one," her mother commented, placing her hand on Azalea's shoulder. She nearly jumped out of her skin, not realising she was no longer alone. "When even was that from?"

Azalea looked at the photo, trying to remember. In the picture, she was perched between her mother and Poppy, all of their tongues stuck out. Poppy looked so happy. Life before Hunter, Poppy had always seemed that way.

"How are you coping, my love?" her mother asked, kissing her lightly on the top of her head. Azalea just shrugged. She didn't even know. She just felt weird.

"You'll get there," her mother encouraged, giving her shoulder a tight squeeze. "Ready for counselling?" Azalea nodded, rising to her feet.

With what day it was she, her mother and Lily had all agreed it was for the best to move their session for the week. She'd even agreed that her mother could sit in so that they were all on the same page with her mental health status. None of them wanted a repeat of her suicide attempt, especially with someone else's suicide making her feel like this. Azalea didn't feel she was that low though. She was low, sure, but she didn't think she could be at that point again. She now knew how much it hurt to be on the other end of a suicide note and she hated it. As they made their way to the counsellor's office, Azalea knew it was time to let her mother in. As much as she could handle that day anyway. It would take time for her to let her mother completely in.

A wave of nausea spread through Azalea. It was weird, sitting in the beige waiting room as the clock ticked away on the wall, her mother glued to her side. She didn't know what to expect when they both sat in her safe space. Would she sit by and just listen? Would she be quiet and patient, or would her opinions come flying out like a swarm of wasps? Her nerves were making her itchy. She had the overwhelming feeling to pull at her fingers, yanking any speck of loose skin free. She couldn't help but wonder if her mother felt the same when from the corner of her eye she caught her mother's tapping feet. Her mother's face may have been straight, but her anxiety was blatantly ever present. Her feet were thumping as much as a beating heart.

As the clock stuck 7, Lily's head popped out from behind the door.

"You ready?" she asked, looking between Azalea and her mother. Her mother rose to her feet as Azalea mumbled agreement, getting herself up and following them reluctantly into the session room. Part of her wanted to run away, but she knew she had no choice. She'd agreed to this and now it was time to get it over and done with.

She flopped herself down in the lumpy seat closest to Lily. Unlike the reception and waiting area, the session rooms were full of colour, every room themed. This was the third one they'd used and it was one of her favourites. It was filled to the brim with galactic prints with a mash-up of purples and blues together with stars and constellations. She knew the rooms were done up for the younger kids, which saddened her just to think about, but the colours and themes helped to calm her. It helped her mind to wander as she talked to the prettier things in the world and with her mind no longer focused on the words leaving her mouth, she found she could be completely honest. She wasn't pretending to be whole anymore. She was just being her true self.

"How are we today, ladies?" Lily smiled sweetly as she sat across from them, notebook and pen already perched on her lap.

"Yeah, we're okay, I think?" Her mother answers questionably, eyebrow arched as she looked Azalea's way.

Azalea nodded. "It's not been great, but it's been bearable," she agreed. "I expected it to be a lot worse, honestly." She shrugged, looking down at her hands. She knew she had to be completely honest here. She was always honest in these sessions with Lily. She couldn't treat her mother being here any different.

"Have you spoken to your mother about what we do here, Azalea, or do you want me to explain?" Lily waited patiently for Azalea's answer. She knew after a few sessions of working with her that she could take quite a while to respond with things she found difficult.

"Can you explain?" Azalea asked. She didn't know how to word it right and she didn't want to confuse her mother.

"Well," Lily smiled at Azalea's mother, tapping her pen against her notebook, "In these sessions, we cover whatever Azalea is feeling at that time. Recently, we've covered grief a fair amount but that's understandable with everything that has gone on in the last year." Looking between Azalea and her mother, Lily opened the notebook. "Are we ready to begin today's session?"

Azalea smiled back sadly. "Yes, we are." She reached out and took her mother's hand in her own. She squeezed, trying to reassure her mother. She was well and truly ready for this. It had taken a while to get to this point, but she was finally there. Ready to bear her life to the person who gave it to her.

It may have only been an hour session, but it felt like they spoke for hours. Azalea let her guard down, finally allowing herself to be freed from the dungeon she had locked herself in. She was acting like her very own villain and it was time to change. She opened up about her feelings and for the first time in a long time, she felt listened to. Not just from her counsellor, from her mother as well. She felt like she was finally able to let her mother in. There was tears and lots of them.

When the clock's hand finally struck 8, she felt lighter. She emerged from the room a near completely different woman, with the red, swollen eyes to prove it. Her mother seemed to feel the same, with her own blood shot set.

Epilogue

This time last year, she still had a sister. She was going to be an aunt. She was going to college to study politics. She was already running through her university choices in her mind. There were so many opportunities ahead of her; she just had to follow where her head took her. She could have been anything back then. But now, all of that was gone. Today was going to be long, miserable and practically unliveable.

The counselling session with her mother had helped them get into the somewhat right place together. They'd been able to decide what they wanted to do to get their minds off the anniversary. Instead of mourning, they'd spend the day celebrating together. Today was a mother/daughter day, even if to the rest of the world it was Halloween.

Azalea's love for the holiday wasn't quite there this year. The part of her heart that had always loved the orange and black colours, excitedly watched the psychological thrillers playing in the local cinema, stuffed her face with the themed candies, had been long since buried for good. She'd finally grown out of the holiday and lived the thriller. She didn't need that world anymore. Her reality was more important, even if she did still get a slight twinge to dance along to the Monster Mash as it played in the supermarket, the MJ zombie arms ready to swing wild. She hurried her shopping along and quickly paid after grabbing the prettiest bouquet of flowers she could see.

Walking outside, she made her way to her mother's side. Without a word, she handed the flowers over and took her hand. They walked side by side, no words left to be said. Not at that point. They both were filled with dread, knowing where their feet were heading. One step in front of the other, their feet led them to the cemetery's gates, perched slightly open by a crumbling brick. One foot at a time, they made their way to where Poppy lay. Standing over the headstone, her head rested on her mother's shoulder.

"You were right about the headstone, you know," her mother said, staring down at it. "She wouldn't have liked my choice. Not exactly a choice a mother ever thinks she will need to make though."

"I know, mum, I know," Azalea nodded, "but you're wrong. Poppy would have loved this." She tapped her foot against the headstone, "Of course it wouldn't have been her number one choice, but you know Poppy. She wouldn't have cared either way as long as her name was all over it and she knew you put your heart into it."

She heard a whimper from her mother's direction and wrapped her arm around her waist, giving her a tight squeeze. "You've still got me, mum. I'm not going anywhere."

Her mother cried harder at that, a laugh escaping with the tears. "Oh darling, if I could wrap you up in bubble wrap and protect you from the world right now, I would. But that's not living, not for either of us."

It had been a week since their joint session with Lily, but Azalea could tell that they both felt better. It wasn't going to be exactly like it was before, but they could get close. There was something between them that hadn't been there over the last year and they just needed to let it rise. A family, teasing type of love that had been hidden away behind their mutual grief.

Her mother bent down and lay the flowers down on the headstone. Before standing fully, she kissed the headstone. Azalea felt tears welling in her eyes, but she knew it was okay. She had to accept that her grief for Poppy would always be there, but she knew she could deal with it when it came down to it. For the first time, Azalea didn't feel the need to stand around and speak to the dead. If she needed someone to talk to, she had a living mother willing to listen to all the problems that came her way.

With their lights on low and a horror movie in the background to keep from trick or treaters knocking on their front door, Azalea's mind was running wild. She'd been thinking about it all day. Part of her life would always be incomplete, but she wanted to change that. Poppy may be gone, but she knew she had more family out there. She just had to find out where. She had to ask. She couldn't hold in her curiosity anymore.

"Mum, it's time." It felt like Azalea had been holding her breath for most of her life, too scared to press her mother any further, but after everything that she'd been through in the last year she decided she needed to start to live her life, no matter what the risk could be. "I want to know about my dad." She looked intently at her mother. She wasn't going to back down this time. She wanted to meet the man whose DNA formed half of her being. It was finally time to meet her dad.

Life

May not be all that is promised

Or all that is wanted

But it is what we are given

And unfortunately

It is the only hand

We have to play

So live it

To the greatest depths

And let nothing

Stand in your way

Take a deep breathe

And make sure it counts

Because at the end of the day

It is your life to live

No one else's

AUTHOR'S NOTES

I just want to thank all the people who've put up with me and my ramblings about this novel since I started it back in 2017 – My amazing husband Michael; my mother Karen, my brothers Anthony, Nathan and Brandon and my sister in-law Chloe; my grandmother Pamela and aunt Katrina; My in-laws Nadine and Stuart; my sister in-law and brothers-in-law Rebecca, Jonathan and Luke; my best friends Helen, Lily and Antt. You've all pushed me and encouraged me to keep going with your positive feedback and it has meant so much to me, you wouldn't believe.

I'd also like to thank 3 people who are no longer with us – Granville, Myra and Bill – my grandparents. They always pushed me to follow the things I was passionate about and writing and writing definitely fall into that category. I hope I still make them all proud.

This book touches on a lot of emotional, personal subjects – abuse, suicide and drug use amongst other things. I have personal experience with some of the issues I have touched on in this book and I know that it can be hard to ask for help, but when you need it there are many people and services out there to assist you. Mental health is still stigmatised to an extent in 2020 but it is an important issue that needs to be discussed more openly and publicly. If you experienced anything I have written about and have survived to live another day, just know that there are people out there who are proud of you for getting on with your life and it can get better.

Please find information for some of the available services on the next page.

ADDICTION

www.alcoholics-anonymous.org.uk

www.begambleaware.org

www.ukna.org

ALZHEIMER'S SUPPORT

www.alzheimers.org.uk

BEREAVEMENT

www.cruse.org.uk

CARER'S SUPPORT

www.gov.uk/carers-uk

www.ageuk.org.uk

CRIME VICTIMS

www.rapecrisis.org.uk

www.victimsupport.org

DOMESTIC/CHILD ABUSE

www.victimsupport.org.uk

www.cps.gov.uk/domestic-violence

www.nationaldahelpline.org.uk

www.refuge.org.uk

www.nspcc.org.uk

MENTAL HEALTH

www.mind.org.uk

www.mentalhealth.org.uk

www.rethink.org

www.samaritans.org.uk

www.sane.org.uk/support

www.papyrus-uk.org

www.youngminds.org.uk

Printed in Poland
by Amazon Fulfillment
Poland Sp. z o.o., Wrocław